Homeland

ISBN: 1-4609-1915-7
ISBN-13: 9781460919156

Homeland

A Vietnam War Story of the Montagnards

Y-Danair B Niehrah
Cover design or artwork by H'Liana Niehrah

Dedication

To my grandfather, Y-Thih Eban Buôn Kang, who's body has never been found..

Acknowledgements

I thank God my Savior for everything.

My teachers who scolded me when I sat down at the computer to write: Rene Miles, Mary-Ann Henry, Sean Scapellato, and Francis Hammes. Without them, I'd still be writing stories about ninjas and aliens. My mentor John Thompson, who shared a plethora of knowledge and experience with me.

The whole 2011 Creative Writing Class—for being great writers, great people, and great friends—and for putting up with me for seven years. For all of my friends, who have never turned their back on me.

And most of all, my family—for everything.

PREFACE

Homeland, takes place in the Central Highlands of Vietnam, home to the indigenous Degar, or Montagnards. Throughout the Vietnam War, the Degar played a crucial role serving as scouts and soldiers for the Americans who were determined to regain the highlands.

The French were the first to colonize the Central Highlands of Vietnam. They gave them the name, "Montagnards", which means mountaineers, because they were driven from the fertile coastline by the invading Cham and Vietnamese peoples. France realized the Montagnards' rights of land and defined the borders of Vietnam, giving the Montagnards a right to formalize their own nation. They called the nation the "Pays Montagnards du Sud Indochinois" or The Montagnard Country of South Indochina.

However, after the French left in 1955, the Montagnards began to fight alone for their land. The Vietnamese began to "colonize" the Montagnard lands, calling them "moi" or savages. The Vietnamese desired to have all of the land, interested in its rich resources, most of which lay in the heart of the country— the Central Highlands, the land of the Montagnards.

When the Vietnam War began and the Americans joined, the Montagnards fought alongside them. They gave us the nickname "yards". The Americans promised that if the Montagnards fought alongside them, they'd help return their land.

After years of fighting, in 1975, U.S. Consulate General Moncrief Spear told Edmund Sprague—a steadfast friend of the Montagnards and a Green Beret in the U.S. Army—if things worsened in Vietnam, the U.S. would be there to take care of the Montagnard peoples. At around the same time, Sprague was then assigned to gather the Montagnard peoples on the beaches, where U.S. Navy ships would come for evacuation. It was later revealed that, while American and Vietnamese employees were evacuated to Saigon, the plan to evacuate the Montagnards had been canceled.

On April 2, 1975, Sprague met with U.S. Ambassador Martin and requested U.S. Navy ships to evacuate the Montagnards. Martin said that the U.S. had higher priorities, and that it could not be done. Sprague told Martin that the blood of thousands of Montagnards would be on his hands.

On April 4, 1975, a large meeting was called into order. Several Montagnard leaders, such as Ksor Rot and Nay Luett, met with Edmund Sprague, Colonel Lamar Prosser, and Special Assistant to Ambassador Martin, Mr. Jacobson. Minister Nay Luett made a plea for U.S. support so they could continue to fight the North Vietnamese until South Vietnam could regroup and U.S. reinforcements could return. Mr. Jacobson told him the U.S. priority was to evacuate the Vietnamese, who were classified as "Political Refugees", as the Montagnards were not. He bluntly told the Montagnard leaders that the South Vietnamese government would only defend Saigon, and not the Central Highlands.

When U.S. troops left and Vietnam fell under communist rule, the Montagnards faced endless torture and killings, which still goes on today. Their land is scarred with churches that have been burned to the ground, and several important Montagnard figures have gone missing and never heard from again. The Human Rights Watch said, "The Montagnards have been repressed for decades," and yet nothing has been done.

The Montagnards still suffer today. According to Dr. Gerald C. Hickey, who wrote *Sons of the Mountains*, over 200,000 of the estimated one million Montagnard peoples have been killed, and 85% of their villages destroyed or abandoned. The lives of the Montagnards have been shattered, and the existence of their culture is rapidly diminishing.

My father grew up in the middle of the war, fighting to survive since he was just a child. He often tells me about life back home—cliff diving from the top of waterfalls, riding on the backs of elephants and feeling the vibration of Vietnamese artillery run up his bones. This is his story.

1

When I was young, there was a river called Eatam that ran through my village. I don't think it could be called a river now. I sit here today and look out over the Charleston harbor; watch factories spew out thick clouds of smoke, watch the blue waters become murky and dark.

My son tossed a plastic bottle out the window of our car once, off the Ravenel Bridge.

He rolled up his window and looked at me. "What?"

"I should make you fetch it out," I told him.

"Why does it matter?"

I grimaced. I wanted to tell him to appreciate the things God had given him, but instead, I said, "I remember back home..."

May 2, 1962

The dry soil sifted between my toes as I stepped out the longhouse. Shouts of children echoed through the jungle as they ran to follow the adults toward the river. The sun was out that day; blistering and humid. The air smelled like spices and herbs; fish and boiled vegetables.

I jogged behind the line of children and watched my uncle's broad shoulders bob up and down, brushing against bamboo leaves. He sat on the back of an elephant, his legs dangling in front of its flapping ears. The beast played its trunk's trumpet wildly, the noise piercing the air. I left small footprints compared to the elephants, as I pushed through the crowd of villagers and slid behind the beast. I wanted to shout at my uncle and ask if I could hop on with him, but the beast stopped.

Icy water wrapped around my feet and mingled in between my toes. I was only six at this time, but even then I could understand the beauty of the river. The clear water danced in the sun's rays. Fish scurried in between rocks, their colorful scales shimmering.

"Fish!" My younger cousin, Y-Duar grabbed at the water with his hands, catching nothing but the rocks at the bottom. The fish slipped between idle fishing poles and tried darting upstream. "Y-Ben, catch it!" He yelled to me.

I followed the fish as it crept along the edge of the riverbed. It closed its mouth around a drifting worm and began to tug, but it couldn't move. My eldest cousin, and closest friend, Y-Yôhan yanked his bamboo pole behind his head. Y-Duar's eyes never left the fish as it flopped onto the flat rock bed, twisting and yanking at the hook before its fins draped down over its dying body.

Y-Yôhan grinned as he unhooked the fish and stuffed it into his bag tied around his tanned shoulders. A copper necklace dangled from his neck, the gemstones on it glimmering green and purple in sun. He had it for as long as I can remember—a gift from our grandfather. "Hey,Y-Ben!"

I walked over to him, my feet brushing against the grainy river bed. "Hey, how many have you caught?"

"Tons!" He grinned. He always grinned. "Have you ever helped with the *nao yao?*"

"No...what is it?" I asked. The rushing water splashed cold against my legs.

Y-Yôhan grabbed my shoulder and slapped a bamboo basket over my head. He was four years my elder, and took advantage of it at every moment.

"Come on, I'll show you." He started down the shallow part of the river, where the crystalline water met the elephant's thunderous feet. He tossed his fishing pole onto the shore where younger children sat, watching with wide eyes. He turned to look at me. "Hurry up!"

The elephant roared, spewing a geyser of water from its trunk. It reared on its hind legs before shaking the earth with a crash as it came down. The ripples and waves in the water exhausted the swarming fish, and they rose to the surface. Y-Yôhan quickly waddled down in the water and snatched two or three fish with his basket.

My uncle slowly guided the elephant through the deeper parts of the river, the water rippling from the massive animal. It rose up to the elephant's neck, but it didn't seem to mind. "Come, come!" he said. Men who were already in the river scooped up the fish that floated on the surface with baskets and nets. It wasn't long before I was competing with Y-Yôhan to try and capture the most fish.

That was *nao yao*, a fragment of my childhood—a forgotten memory.

Villagers soon began to pack their baskets of fishing supplies, and several others helped lift heavy nets of fish. The elephants slowly and noisily trotted through the mud and brush. I stayed behind with Y-Yôhan to help carry his large basket.

"It's too heavy!" he groaned. He began to drag it, leaving a long streak in the muddy soil. "Stupid fish…"

A glimpse back at the river distracted me. A large fish swept down the river, its pale body floating above the surface, its fins torn. Soon after, debris and trash followed—bottles, large strips of plastic and cardboard.

"Look," I said, pointing to the river. The trash had already floated down, and Y-Yôhan only shrugged.

He dragged his catch of fish toward the village, but I stayed for a few moments longer. A man appeared from the other side of the river, a rifle hanging loosely at his hip from a leather strap. He watched me, lips curled around his cigarette. He wore black pajamas, buttoned at the collar. I wanted to say something, but he flicked his cigarette into the river, and left.

"What are you looking at?" Y-Yôhan asked. "I need your help with this."

I took my eyes off the river and walked over to help. I kept looking back, hoping to see the man again. But all I saw was the trash and fish that floated limp down the river. Dead.

The horizon faded to a soft orange and red. The sun's glow fell over the edge of the mountains. Cool winds swept down from the heights, blowing between my fingers as I sat down beside my father and brother. My father held a guitar in his hands, strumming the chords the French missionaries taught him. The people danced and cheered happily, their bodies swaying to the paling sky above them as the flames from the bonfire licked at their swirling shadows.

"Dad?"

My father handed the guitar to his brother. The music continued. He looked at me and smiled. "Yes?"

"Will we do the *nao yao* again?"

His pause before answering me made me curious. "Of course, why not?"

"Because the fishes are dying…" I told him.

He did what he always did when he didn't know what to say. He cracked his knuckles and cleared his throat. "Nothing lives forever."

His brother handed the guitar back, and my father began strumming it again. His eyes were solemn, the flames crafting a yellow glow into his eyes.

I saw a man by the river too. He had a rifle strapped to his hip and a cigarette pressed against his lips.

I don't know why I didn't tell him. Maybe I thought it didn't matter. Maybe it was the look of happiness on everyone's faces that caused me to hold my tongue. But perhaps, if I said something, we would've had more time.

2

"Jake's picking me up soon." I heard my son stomp down the stairs, his keychain dangling noisily from his hip.

"For?" I turned the volume down on the television and brought a mug of coffee to my lips.

"We're watching Nightmare on Elm Street."

"That old thing?"

"It's a remake," he grinned. "You said the original was scary?"

"Not really," I replied, resting the mug on the small glass coffee table in front of me.

"C'mon, you've got to be scared of something."

I laughed.

July 20, 1963

I will never forget the day I stared down the dirt-caked barrel and saw the copper bullet resting in the chamber. My toes were clenched around the gravel on the road. I couldn't stop my hands from shaking. I licked the insides of my mouth, running my tongue over dry walls. Behind the gun, the man bent the lit cigarette in his mouth. The large boar that rested on his shoulder dripped red.

Thirty minutes before, we sat perched upon a bed of rocks and mud, the smooth wood of our crossbows resting in our palms. Our eyes scanned the trees and the jungle floor for small game: foxes, rabbits, squirrels. But the jungle was eerily still. The sunlight dotted the morning soil, passing between the swaying bamboo leaves. It was wet. The monsoon clouds would be coming back in a couple of days, and this was the time to hunt.

I had gotten used to the rain. I think we all had. I was always paranoid of leeches during these times. I never knew they were attached to my arm or leg until they fell off. If some of my older cousins or uncles were around, they'd burn the leeches off with the tip of their cigarette. "A waste," my cousins would always say. "Dry cigarettes are precious."

Y-Yôhan led our group of four, along with his two brothers of the same age, Y-Tom and Y-Alain. I slung my crossbow over my shoulder and leaned against the bark of a tree.

"How long are we going to wait?" I asked.

"Yeah, we've been sitting here for at least an hour..." Y-Tom groaned.

"I told you not to complain." Y-Yôhan began with a grin. "If you want to leave, you can hike by yourself back to the village."

I sighed. "Fine, but tell us what you're doing."

"I'm waiting for deer...or...something..." he turned to us. "Don't tell me you guys aren't tired of monkeys or rabbits, or snakes..."

"I don't care," Y-Alain said, exhausted. "If it takes hours to catch a deer, I don't care."

After a brief moment of silence, Y-Yôhan mounted a bolt onto his crossbow. We tensed up, hands reaching for our own, and quickly followed him as he began to creep down the jungle slopes.

He put a finger to his lips and waved Y-Tom over to him. They spoke softly. Y-Tom grinned when Y-Yôhan pointed in the distance. They started off again, Y-Alain and I sticking close behind, our crossbows lowered to the ground, the quiver of bolts on our back swaying. Our pace quickened to a jog, Y-Yôhan shuffled through brush cautiously, his eyes never leaving the target in the distance.

Our feet patted softly against the mud. We stopped just outside of a small clearing. Sunlight enveloped the floor. A family of rabbits scurried across the grass and leaves into their burrow. In the midst of the clearing, a large boar stood, poking at grubs in the soil. I remember looking at the long, curved tusks of the boar, stained with grime.

Aggressive little things. Ama, or father, said once. They might've been, but, better to find a boar than a tiger.

"It's huge." Y-Alain grinned. He aimed his crossbow at the animal, finger steady on the wooden trigger. The boar turned to face us, squealing loudly. Y-Alain pulled the trigger, surprised, and the bolt caught the boar in its muscular shoulder. It yelped and darted off, the bolt jutting out, blood seeping from the wound.

"Get it!" Y-Yôhan said, firing his crossbow. The bolt splintered a tree beside the boar, but the beast luckily got away.

I never got to fire my crossbow that day. We soon lost track of the boar, but Y-Yôhan was determined, following blood tracks. "It's around here, some-where," he said.

"We're not going to find it," Y-Alain said. "Let's catch a monkey or something and go home."

"No, we're finding that boar!" Y-Yôhan said. "Y-Ben, don't you want to eat something else?"

I stretched and yawned. "I really don't care."

"Of course you do!" he said for me.

We heard a loud *pop* that made birds squawk and flutter from their branches. The tree leaves rustled. Y-Yôhan led us forward. We were all tense, our fingers on the trigger. I had the impression that perhaps one of our older cousins found it and shot it with one of the guns the Americans gave to us. But as we came across a dirt path, the boar lay on the ground, a hole in it's head. We stood over its body.

"What are you doing?" A voice asked in Vietnamese.

I looked up and found myself face to face with the cold brown eyes of a soldier and froze. He casually wielded a pistol in his right hand, the orange tip of a cigarette glowing between his lips. A funny green helmet rested on his head, and he was clothed head to toe in green fatigues.

He towered over me, and I stepped back as he picked up the boar and slung it over his shoulder. The way he twirled the pistol in one hand, and the way his scarred lips curled as he grinned was unnerving.

"What are *you* doing?" Y-Yôhan ran to the front of our group, approach-ing the man with his hands planted firmly on the stock of his crossbow. "That's ours!"

"So?" The man chuckle, almost growling. Y-Yôhan reached for the boar, but found the butt of the man's pistol. I watched my cousin crumple to the ground, and instinctively, we drew our crossbows, the tip of our bolts pointing at the man's throat.

He eyed over our weapons curiously before taking another drag on the cigarette. A puff of smoke seeped from his nostrils as he asked, "What are you going to do with those toys?"

He pointed the pistol at my head, obscuring my vision with the dark-ness of the barrel. I heard a click, and realized it was my finger resting on the wooden trigger of my crossbow. My eyes never left the barrel of the gun, nor the man's cold eyes. His grin faded into a scowl when he realized he had two other weapons turned on him.

"Go back to your houses." He lowered the pistol and began to walk away. "*Moi.*"

Savages.

The sun was resting between a stretch of clouds, casting a faint glow on our backs. We slumped toward the village, dragging our feet. We had a quiver full of bolts, and no catch to eat. Y-Yôhan was quiet; his head bent low, eyes shifting over the scorched soil in front of him. He was holding the side of his head, where blood had caked.

We walked into the village, greeted by other friends who immediately joked and asked where the "big game" Y-Yôhan kept talking about, was. While Y-Alain and Y-Tom were left to explain, Y-Yôhan and I walked to my longhouse, where my father sat on the porch with my uncle.

My father's grin faded from his aging face as he saw us slump up the steps. My uncle waved out his hand and asked, "Where have you guys been?"

We walked into the house—I rested my crossbow against the wall and felt a hand on my shoulder.

Whenever my father wanted to talk, he had a funny way of expressing it. He would never try to be soft or sympathetic—my cousins would always get "hey what's wrong" or "are you alright". My father said, "Talk."

I hesitated, and looked at Y-Yôhan, who sat cross legged on a bamboo mat, back pressed against the wall of the longhouse. He was still holding his head.

"What happened?" His voice, so solemn—he wasn't asking a question, he was demanding an answer.

"*Yuán.*" Vietnamese. Y-Yôhan sighed and moved his hand away from his head; the small cut had stopped bleeding.

My father paused and then cleared his throat. He crossed his arms and stood straight. "Stay here." His brows furrowed as he looked at Y-Yôhan's cut, but he didn't speak of it. He left abruptly, saying *come* to his brother, who shot up from the wooden chair.

Soon after my mother and aunt barged into the room, screaming about the rodent that had snuck underneath the longhouse.

"Well get one of the men to get it out!" Y-Yôhan's mother said frantically waving her arms. "I don't want that thing to crawl into the house!"

She stopped by Y-Yôhan and looked at his head. "Ahh, my poor baby, what happened?" Y-Yôhan groaned and rolled his eyes as she grabbed his cheeks and looked at the wound.

"Stop it, stop it." Y-Yôhan he frowned. "That hurts!"

"Of course it does—getting yourself into trouble again when your father told you not to." She sucked her teeth.."…never listen…"

My *ami*, or mom, stood silent, hands on her hip—a wooden cooking spoon in her other hand. "*Yuán?*"

I nodded. Y-Yôhan's mother frowned and looked him in the eye. "Tell me."

I sat quietly as Y-Yôhan explained—our trek for "big game", the boar—the confrontation with the Vietnamese soldier. I noticed how he hesitated when he said he was hit by the soldier—the concerned faces of his mother and mine biting their lips.

"I have to talk to your father about this; you stay in the village, no more hunting!"

"I'll get some ice for him." Ami said. They left the longhouse in a rush, their timid bodies scurrying across the jungle floor over to the other huts.

Y-Yôhan shook his head and closed his eyes. "What's going on…"

"I don't know…"

I peeked outside the longhouse. No cool wind swept down from the mountain tops. The trees were still. The animals silent. And yet the monsoon clouds were drawing ever closer to our village.

I don't know…

3

It wasn't always tough. Y-Yôhan was always leading us into trouble, and everyone else was always taking the blame. We never pointed a finger at him. We never tried covering it up. Because in the end, no one cared.

My son asked me once what I do for fun, and I didn't know how to answer him. I told him, "Solitaire" or, "Working" though he knew the latter was a lie. Unsatisfied, he started upstairs to his room. I stopped him. "Want to know what I did for fun back home?"

He groaned and slumped into a chair next to the television. "Sure, Dad."

August 12, 1962

I was unaware that the war had already started. I had just turned seven, days earlier.

There was always something new to do; Y-Yôhan made sure of that. Monsoons had passed, and Y-Yôhan was dragging me out of the village to a nearby waterfall called Drai Sap.

We were barefoot, hopping over roots and brush. We both carried a walking stick in one hand and a dagger in the other, protection against snakes and wild boars. The jungle was loud. Birds perched high in trees splintered by lightning. The rush of nearby streams flooded our ears.

"Come on, don't be a wuss," Y-Yôhan chuckled. "They're waiting for us at the top." Teasing was in his nature. He rarely took anything seriously.

"I'm not!" I was falling behind. Constantly lifting my feet out of inches of mud and carrying the long walking stick began to take its toll. My arms and legs ached, but every step I took, the sounds of the waterfall grew louder.

A little further, you can rest there. Besides, stop now, and you'll have everyone else calling you a wuss. I gathered what little strength I had left and pushed my way to the top of a steep hill that led to the waterfall. I heard Y-Yôhan push on ahead and exchange playful comments with the rest of our cousins.

The water seemed to glow in the sunlight. Fish scurried between smooth, pale rocks at the top, and the water had risen dramatically because of the monsoon. The water clashing against the rocks at the bottom of the falls seemed to drown out most noise, except for my cousins, who spun and flipped, and howled in laughter when one landed flat on his or her belly.

"Ready to jump?" one of my cousins, Y-Đavid asked.

I guess Y-Yôhan caught the look of terror I had on my face. Maybe he saw my legs shaking as I stood looking out over the misty water.

"It just looks far, it's nothing." Y-Yôhan grinned.

I shifted uneasily. It was hard trying to act as if the thought of plummeting into rocks didn't bother me.

"Just don't miss." Y-Đavid winked as he flipped to the water below.

"He's just trying to scare you." Y-Yôhan set his walking stick and knife on the rocks next to the crest of the falls. He unhooked his sparkling necklace and set it down on top of his shirt. "Don't worry about it."

I watched him leap off the top of the rocks—screaming all the way down—and crash far from where the end of the waterfall met the water. *Don't worry about it.*

The sun shot into my eyes like a spear as I stood up on the rocks. My skin was goose bumped from the cool breeze. Everyone below was shouting at me to jump. Y-Yôhan was silent, almost impassive, except for a slight grin when I stepped to the edge.

The oldest and loudest of the group was H'Rmak. She was from the Jarai tribe, the largest of the Montagnards, while we lived within the Rahde tribe, the second largest.

"Come on!" she shouted through cupped hands. "Let's go!"

The others followed her chants and grew louder. My ears grew hot as I stood straight. The large pool of water looked miniscule from the top of the falls. The crashing water suddenly began to take over the shouts. I focused on the water below me and took a breath. My stomach to lurched. Sweat slid down my cheeks and fell onto my rough toes.

I envisioned my body sprawled out on the rocks, my head cracked open by a jagged rock near the waterfall. I imagined slipping, body flailing in the air. But I heard them screaming, shouting. I saw their arms waving, their faces smiling. *Jump.*

So I did. My chest grew light, and my legs and arms flailed wildly. The wind whistled through my ears before I struck the surface of the mountain's pool. I couldn't find the bottom of the pool, but felt my legs thrashing in the icy cold. The surface was warmer, and I quickly rose, gasping for a breath.

I was greeted to cheers and "woo hoos". Y-Yôhan slapped me hard on my back. I rubbed my eyes and blew my nose.

"See, it's easy," Y-Yôhan said, and then added, "Round two!"

———————

We had to walk several miles to school, maybe four or five at the least. My parents always wanted us to travel in a group, for protection. I never knew from what. My mother wouldn't elaborate on the subject, instead she'd just say, "Stop arguing with me", and slap my behind with a wooden spoon.

Y-Yôhan and my other cousins joined me; four or five of us most of the time. Sometimes my older cousins would let me sit on their shoulders. We were always loud, stomping and shouting, loud enough for the birds to flee from the trees that surrounded the dirt path to the school. I'd notice strange tracks in the dirt sometimes. "Jeeps and tanks", my cousins would say. I never saw any.

All of our classes were in French. I learned it at the same rate as my native tongue. My cousins and I were always the loudest ones in our class, not to mention the craftiest. I remember our teachers briskly walking in shouting, "*Tais toi!*" and the whole class would go silent.

We took a detour off the main path one day after school. It was Y-Yôhan , Y-Alain, H'Rmak, and I—and we all needed to relieve ourselves. Each of us found trees to take care of our business, and when we were done, we met back up on the main path. We waited for Y-Yôhan, but he never showed.

We stood there silently, before H'Rmak and Y-Alain began to walk away.

"Whatever, he knows the way home." H'Rmak said.

I crossed my arms and said, "I'm going to go with Y-Yôhan."

"Sure," H'Rmak said.

I ran after Y-Yôhan. Our home was just another mile further, so finding our way back would be no problem. I hopped over a small creek with small stones and picked up two and weighed them in my hand. I took my slingshot from my back pocket and loaded it, imitating the low stance I had seen my uncles crouch into when they hunted. I pretended I was as good of a hunter as they, poking my head from behind trees and shooting the stones at invisible game.

Y-Yôhan spotted me from a distance and sucked his teeth, producing an odd, yet sharp whistling noise.

"What?" I asked, walking up to him.

"I don't know where my bag is!" he swore and searched the ground, then looked up at me, "Did you guys hide it?"

"Nope!" I shrugged. "Were you even carrying a bag?"

"Yeah." Y-Yôhan grimaced. "That had all my homework in it. And my necklace, too."

Then, a screech echoed from above us. The leaves rustled in the trees, and a second later, a piece of paper fell in between us. We both looked up, and saw a monkey, its skin a dark charcoal, its face a tan and white mix. Its mouth was open as it picked out papers from Y-Yôhan's bag, which was resting in a small nook in the tree. I watched as it screeched again, and ripped another paper in to shreds.

"A monkey!" I was excited. Y-Yôhan, furious, snatched the slingshot from my hand and loaded it with a stone. He held his breath and aimed, just as the monkey pulled out more schoolwork from the bag. Excited, the monkey jumped up and down, causing Y-Yôhan's shot the miss by inches, the rock flying into trees in the distance. I watched the monkey rip up the papers, screaming and shouting. Y-Yôhan's face darkened, and angered, he took aim a second time.

It was the monkey's lucky day. It scurried just as Y-Yôhan fired, fleeing up higher onto a branch above, continuing to rip up papers and chew on them. It pulled out Y-Yôhan's necklace from the bag and eyed it curiously. Y-Yôhan went ballistic. He found a rock lying under a bed of fallen leaves, and juggled it in his palm. He loaded the large stone against the elastic band, aiming an inch higher than where the monkey was, and as he fired, the monkey jumped— straight into the rock. The beast caught it directly between the eyes. It yelped and fell onto a branch, then continued down into a bed a leaves, where Y-Yôhan smashed its head in for good measure.

"Stupid...monkey," he repeated as he kicked the body of the animal. He put his necklace back on and began gathering up his papers, but most were torn to shreds. "What am I supposed to say?"

I shrugged. "Should we get the bag?"

Y-Yôhan looked up the tree to where the bag was resting high upon one of the branches, the strap hooked onto several smaller branches. The smooth tree had no low branches to hang from, neither did it have vines. "There's no way we can get up there. Ugh, all my teachers are going to kill me," he kicked the dirt on top of one of the scraps of paper. "So is my *ama* and *ami*..."

When we returned back to the village, Y-Yôhan went straight to my home, where his father was, as always, sharing a pot of freshly brewed coffee with Ama. Y-Yôhan's father, Y-Puih watched us walk in. I was smiling, though I didn't know why. I didn't like seeing Y-Yôhan in trouble, but I have to admit I was excited to see how he'd squirm out of this one. The bags were time consuming to knit and sew, taking days to finish a flawless one. The embroidery and intricate designs Y-Yôhan had on his bag might've taken weeks to complete—that was my reasoning to why he was so upset over it.

Y-Yôhan tried walking past them at first. He made it to the backroom before his father called from the kitchen. "Aren't you missing something?"

"No?" Y-Yôhan answered back, looking down the hall. He cracked his knuckles and cleared his throat. He was sweating.

"Your bag." Y-Puih said, his voice rumbling. "Where is it?"

Y-Yôhan didn't answer.

"Come here." His father said. Y-Yôhan sluggishly went into the kitchen. I watched from the hallway.

"Yes?" Y-Yôhan's eyes were on the ground.

"You lost it?" Y-Puih asked, then added, "look at me."

"Yes," he replied.

"The monkey—" I stopped when Y-Yôhan shot me a menacing glare.

"Monkey?" Ama's lips curled into a grin. "A monkey stole your bag?" He broke out into a hard laugh. Y-Puih even cracked a slight smile. "You're not finding that."

"The monkey ripped up all the papers," Y-Yôhan continued, the smiles on his father's face easing the tension away. "But we smashed its head in!"

"Did you at least bring it back?" Y-Puih sat back down and took a sip from his mug.

"It was all...squished," I said.

"Not that, the bag!" Ama said.

"It was too high up the tree—and there was no way we could climb it," Y-Yôhan said.

Ama cleared his throat after a slight chuckle and then shook his head. "Well, you can't do much about that. Monkeys are the most two-faced animal on this planet—they'll be nice one second, then steal your stuff for no reason."

"Why?" I didn't understand why a dumb little creature would walk away with something so useless to them, like school papers.

"It's just their nature," Ama shrugged. "Just like it is mans' nature to save himself."

"I wouldn't say that's true," Y-Puih leaned back in his chair and rested his hands on the back of his head. "There are some unselfish people out there."

"Not when people are shooting at you," Ama said.

"Huh?" Y-Yôhan sat down. "Who's shooting?"

"Never mind." Y-Puih took a sip from his coffee. "Go play outside, I'll get you another bag tonight."

Y-Yôhan and I left the house. He told me he was going to go back to his home for a nap. I watched him leave and then headed back to my house, but I stopped at the door and crouched low, a thin wall of wood and bamboo between Ama and I.

"They're getting restless," Y-Puih said.

"Well so am I." Ama cleared his throat. "You know they're slowly getting more forces."

"Well what should we do?"

"I'm not sure." I heard the chairs slide against the floorboards and I backed off behind the house. They walked past me and out into the village, the last thing I heard being, "but we better start getting ready."

———

Y-Yôhan and I went to shoot our slingshots with some of our older cousins the next morning. I watched them stick the handle of the spear into the dirt and mount a hollowed rock on top of it, like a helmet.

"What are we doing?" I asked.

"Shooting the rocks, if you break it, you win," Y-Yôhan said, stretching the band on his slingshot.

We took turns firing the slingshots. My left arm was quivering as I tugged on the elastic band with all my strength. I thought it was going to snap. My rock spiraled through the air and struck the fence behind the spears. It collided with a loud *thunk* and landed on the dirt. Y-Yôhan fired directly after, grinning like an idiot as his rock went through one end of the rock and out the other.

It was when they replaced the rocks that I stopped playing. I couldn't go on. I watched one of my cousins grab something wrapped in a red towel and walk over to the spear jutting out of the ground. He rested it on top of the shaft. It was a skull, with cracks running down the side of the eye socket. Y-Yôhan must've seen it too, I guess, because when I looked around, I couldn't find him.

"Going to shoot first?" My cousin asked me.

I shook my head.

"Aw, come on, it's just a stupid Vietcong," he laughed.

I left and found Y-Yôhan sitting alone at home sanding his crossbow. I watched him work; we were both silent. I lit a few candles when the sun set behind the jagged mountains, and when he finished, I finally broke the silence.

"What do you think they were talking about?" I stretched myself over the bamboo mats.

He shrugged. "I don't know." He set his crossbow aside, leaning it against the wooden frame of the wall.

"Hey, what's a Vietcong?" I asked him, hoping for an actual reply this time.

He shrugged again. "I don't know—why are you asking me?"

"I don't want to ask *ama*, I'll bet he'd get mad if I did."

"Then don't talk about it," he said suddenly. His eyes were focused on the ground. Not once did he smile ever since we came back inside from shooting our slingshots.

"You wouldn't leave me, would you?" I asked.

He looked up this time, confused. "What do you mean?"

"If we were getting chased by tigers...or...I don't know," I paused. "Like what your dad said, you're not selfish are you?"

"Oh." Y-Yôhan chuckled and put a hand on my head. "Of course not, we're pretty much brothers. But, I don't know, I wouldn't want to get eaten by a tiger."

"Well then, you're a wuss!" I stuck my tongue out at him and he replied by pushing me.

"Hey, how about we make a deal?" He began.

"A deal?"

"Um...a promise."

"Oh, okay," I looked at him, wondering if there was any trick behind this. "What's the promise?"

"I'll look out for you, if you look out for me." Y-Yôhan cracked his knuckles. "You get into a fight, I'll help you, and you do the same for me."

I bit my lip in thought. "Wait, but you're older than me..."

"Well, my dad is seven years older than yours and they both have grey hairs already—I guess it won't matter later on."

"Alright, alright." I nodded. "That sounds good to me, but if you're lying, I get to smack you!"

"Fair!" He stuck out his hand. I looked at it, already torn and callused from the farm equipment. I took the offer and shook.

4

Blood splashed across the screen; limbs flew across bullet-scarred lobbies. Trip mines and explosives sat around each corner. Glows of red flashed on the monitor.

"What's this?" I asked.

My son paused the computer and looked at me, slid the headphones off his ears. "Huh?"

"That's not war."

"It's a game." He turned his volume up so I could hear it through the small speakers of his headphones and put them back on.

If only he knew what war was really like.

June 11, 1968

It was the eve of Chinese New Year. The pale, jungle moon flashed orange and red. I juggled the fireworks in my hands, and watched bright embers explode over the village.

My uncle shouted, "Only a few more hours!" He walked towards me with a wooden box of fireworks in his arms. Sweating, he dropped the crate next to me and smiled. "Take some."

"*Amiet.*" Uncle. I called after him.

"What's up?" He looked at me, put a hand on my head and traced it to his neck. "Wow, you're getting taller, aren't you?"

"I guess." I dug more fireworks out the box while asking, "How long is my dad going to be in Saigon?"

"A few weeks, at the most. Maybe less—it's only a couple of hours from here." He paused. "Can't tell with politics though, Y-Ben."

"Alright." I walked over to the campfire and felt a hard slap on my back, followed by hands grabbing two of the fireworks from beneath my arms.

Y-Yôhan chuckled and stuffed my firework into a custom-made launcher. He lit the fuse, pulled on the launcher's elastic string and released. The rocket spiraled high above us, shattering into a purplish blast that lit up the village. "Woo!" He slapped me with the launcher. "Here, shoot one!"

"I was looking for one of those—thanks for stealing it." I snatched it from his hands and loaded it. "What color?"

"I say...orange!" he shouted over the screams of the other boys and explosions.

"Blue."

"Okay, if it blows up blue I'll..." He paused. "I'll let you shoot my brother's gun."

"Really?" I grinned. "The M60?!"

Y-Yôhan punched my shoulder. "Not the M60, you idiot. The Americans didn't give us any of those...besides you wouldn't be able to lift it."

"Blue." I tapped on the fireworks launcher and ignited the fuse. I pulled back on the band and held it still, counting in my head. Three, two, one—the rocket flew from the barrel, and lit the sky blue with its explosion.

"Knew it!" I pumped my fist in the air and dropped the fireworks and the launcher. "Alright, where's the gun?"

"Not now stupid." Y-Yôhan picked up the fireworks. "Tomorrow, if we go hunting."

"Promise?"

"Sure." He rubbed his large hand through my hair and laughed. "Let's finish these fireworks."

"Alright, but you promised."

He nodded and we shot off the rockets, one after the other, a brilliant display of purple, red, orange, blue filling the calm of the sky.

The night consumed the rest of the fireworks. The only glow was that of the flickering campfire. The flames danced with the shadows and the moonlight. The night was still and almost silent, were it not for the crickets that hummed their melodies in the mountain's cool breeze.

I laid on the mat inside the house, eyes focused on the campfire. I sat up and leaned against the wall, my stomach feeling like it was still picking apart the tender water buffalo we had for dinner.

"Can't sleep either?" Y-Alain lay on his mat, hands behind his head, staring straight up to the moon through a small hole in the roof.

I rubbed my belly and groaned. "They made me eat so much."

"They always do." Y-Alain chuckled. "And they don't even mention dessert until you're so full you're ready to puke."

"Yeah." I stretched. My body ached all over from the long day.

Y-Yôhan walked in the house and collapsed on the floor beside us. We could barely see him through darkness, until he lit a large candle near the entrance. The gems on his pendant glimmered in the darkness. "What are you ladies doing, aren't you supposed to be asleep?"

"Shut up." I laughed.

A sudden explosion shook the longhouse. Pots and vases quivered on top of the tables, and the lit candle toppled over and was extinguished. We heard a high pitched squeal. It was gone almost before it reached our ears.

I looked around, dazed, a smile on my face. "Whoa! That was a huge firework!"

"I thought we shot them all off already." Y-Alain was digging in his ears, trying to shake off the ringing.

I bit my lip as another scream echoed across the village. "Hey, you hear that?"

Y-Yôhan stood up, paused and then signaled for us to follow him. "That's *aê!* Let's go."

We stepped out the house. Villagers and children ran from their homes, carrying their most important belongings in small bags that hung from their shoulders. Aê, or Grandpa, waved his arms, leading a line of quick moving villagers. They were shouting, "Quick, quick, to the bunker!"

Many of the men scoured the homes, checking them in and out for family. Others followed the line of villagers with M16s and AR-15s on their hips, ready to fire at a moment's notice.

"Come, come!" Our grandfather waved his hands at us. We jogged to his side.

"What's going on?" I asked.

Aê grabbed my shoulders and pointed to the bunker across the village. I remember his wide eyes, and the way his usually firm hands were quivering as he held my shoulders. "Not now. Go to the bunker first, go, go." We made our way—all three of us along with the rest of the village into the small bunker. It was cramped, dark, and hot. The walls were cracked already from many years of standing idle, but it was hidden well upon a small hill surrounded by trees.

I wiped sweat off my cheek—I didn't know if it was mine or not. I sat in one of the corners with Y-Alain and Y-Yôhan, who looked around nervously.

I looked around then tapped the shoulder of the woman sitting next to me. "What's going on?"

22

The woman shook her head and stood up to look for her son. She was shaking, and her sleeve was damp with tears.

Y-Yôhan was speaking to his uncle. "The whole thing?" Y-Yôhan asked. His eyes were wide.

"Gone, just like *that*." His uncle snapped his fingers. He had a rifle slung over his shoulder. "An artillery shell hit the missionary bungalow across the highway."

"From who?"

"I don't know—"

My granduncle ran into the bunker, stained with sweat and dirt. "*Yuán, yuán!*" Vietnamese. He struggled to catch his breath as people crowded around him.

"What's going on?" people began to ask.

"*Yuán,* they're crossing the river..." He paused to breathe and pointed at one of the men carrying a rifle. "They have guns."

People began shouting. Saying he was lying.

"I know what I saw!" my great-uncle shouted. "We're not safe here. We should move to the center of Buôn Ma Thuột. It's just down the road. They have more people, more guns."

"We're not moving," a younger man said, his hands on his rifle. "They don't even know this bunker is here."

Everyone shouted over the others, gesturing with their hands and spitting in disgust.

I wiped my quivering palms on my slacks and leaned back against the walls of the bunker, wishing my father was here. Scared.

Dawn came. Sunlight seeped through the cracks of the cement bunker. The villagers awoke to the sounds of gunfire; to explosions and screams. The sounds echoed throughout the jungle—loud, sharp cracks, as if the earth was splitting in two. Most of the villagers were peeking out the bunkers to see what was happening.

I opened my eyes to Y-Alain, pulling me up to my feet.

"They're past our village already—going to the heart of Buôn Ma Thuột," he said. "There's still a few troops left behind to secure the area, but we've been sneaking back to village for supplies."

It was Y-Yôhan's uncle that fired the first shot. Soon after, the rest began firing.

As we stepped outside I had to adjust my eyes in the sun. I heard them shouting to each other, "the chief is dead." Bullets brushed past me, as I ducked low behind the bunker. My knees almost buckled from adrenaline.

"Come with me!" Y-Yôhan said to Y-Alain and I. We moved from the bunker and toward the village. Some villagers were sneaking through the brush and trees and back to their houses. The Vietcong had left the longhouses to burn.

Bodies lay in a revolting pile on the ground. Blood stained the earth beneath our toes. I stood over the body of a woman I knew, who used to give Y-Yôhan and I mung beans steamed in banana leaves when we came to visit. The back of her head was completely blown off. The smell filled my nostrils. It made my stomach turn and I heaved on the ground.

Y-Yôhan led us behind the remains of one of the longhouses. There was a small, rusted shack that seemed to groan as he opened the door.

Y-Yôhan and Y-Alain walked into the shack and returned wielding weapons. Y-Alain had his father's crossbow in his hands, made of their strongest wood—newly strung—with a quiver of bolts strapped to his back. He pulled out a small wooden container and dipped his bolt in the green liquid—a strong poison.

Y-Yôhan shouldered a rifle. An M16. The menacing barrel pointed out into the village. He looked like a professional, the way he flipped it over and blew the dust and sand from the magazine. He cocked the gun and slung the gun over his shoulder with a small leather strap.

I eyed the gun with curiosity.

"Go get your crossbow Y-Ben." Y-Yôhan said.

"I want a gun," I told him.

"There's no more."

"You promised you'd let me shoot the gun."

"Not now. Get your crossbow." He glared at me.

I groaned and grabbed a crossbow from the corner, and fitted the quiver with bolts.

Ducking low and behind the trees and fallen logs, we made our way back to the bunker—Y-Yôhan said it was better to have higher ground. The men were still firing. A few had been hit, blood seeping from wounds. I watched as the men wrap their shirts around their wounds and stood up once more to fire their weapons.

I watched Y-Yôhan's bullets pass through the bamboo leaves and strike a *yuán* dead center, between the eyes. I watched Y-Alain's poisoned bolts strike the soldiers in the neck.

I raised my crossbow for the first time at a human. I felt my hand shake as I gripped the stock tightly, trying to steady my aim. I lined the tip of the bolt with a *yuán,* shut one eye. I held my breath, and hesitated. I watched the man position himself behind a tree away from the main line of fire. The second he looked up at me and aimed brought his weapon up; I snapped the wooden trigger of my crossbow back. The string of tree bark sent the bolt flying.

After the bolt soared straight through the soldier's head and into a tree, I could never go back. The man crumpled to the ground.

I didn't slump down in shock. My knees didn't buckle. My arms didn't go weak. Instead, I reached in my quiver for another bolt and loaded it, pulled the string back and aimed at another.

And another.

———

The fighting continued through the night. In the morning, government officials, led by the South Vietnamese troops, began to evacuate the Montagnards from the Central Highlands, and took them to other bases and stations. I was one of the last ones to leave.

I remembered watching the jeeps veer off down the highway, piles of bodies littering the streets beside them, parents shielding their children from the blood. Death. My arms were sore, my quiver empty, and my hand cramped from gripping my weapon so tightly. I sat alone inside one of the jeeps, my uncles talking to the South Vietnamese soldiers. Y-Yôhan and his father walked over, guns strapped to their bodies.

"How're you doing?" Y-Yôhan asked. His voice was softer than usual, as if the explosions and gunfire had deafened him to the sound of his own voice.

I shook my head. "I don't know..." I felt my throat tighten and took a deep breath. "I don't know."

"It'll be alright," Y-Yôhan said. "We'll be out of here soon—Cambodia, Laos, somewhere safe. Promise."

"Don't promise anything," I remember saying. "You don't have to lie to me."

Y-Yôhan grimaced and then unstrapped his M16. He loaded a new magazine and dropped the gun at my feet. "There."

I looked at it and then back at Y-Yôhan. "Really?"

"Really."

I picked it up and fumbled it in my hands. It was heavier than I thought it'd be. The weight was off. *You shouldn't be able to take so many lives with just eight pounds of metal.*

"I'll teach you how to use it," Y-Yôhan said. "But don't shoot unless you're being shot at, understand?"

"Promise."

The few remaining villagers climbed in the last of the jeeps and set off. The jeep I was in lurched forward and then sped down the dirt road, a cloud of dust trailing behind us. I looked out over dawn's orange horizon and spotted grey clouds of smoke far off in the distance. Jets flew overhead the silver letters on their wings reading "U.S.". The earth rumbled.

5

My son isn't the strongest. He plays video games, writes stories, plays music—never fights or does any sports. I told him once that he'd get beat up by a girl if he didn't start doing something productive. He ran upstairs, muttering under his breath about how annoying I am, and toyed around on his computer.

My father always said when I was younger, that our people were docile. Even so, he and his brothers would teach my cousins and me how to fight; with our bodies, and with weapons

But in my son's world, he doesn't need to know how to fight. He doesn't have to.

June 12, 1968

My ears were ringing. Explosions and gunfire. Helicopters and jets flew overhead, their roars shaking the earth. Every time I lifted my head to look up at the sky, the sun was misshapen by trails of smoke from the burning huts.

Most of the villagers were silent. They seemed haunted. It was in the way they cleaned their muddy clothes and the barrel of their rifles. Tents and makeshift shelters of bamboo and wooden planks were rooted in mud.

The soldiers—Americans, Montagnards, and even some South Vietnamese—spoke about the country. It was falling apart. Bodies littered the Central Highlands, and even the city of Saigon, the South Vietnamese stronghold.

I sat with my cousins in the bed of a large jeep, safe in the center of the village. Most of them had guns strapped to their shoulders. One of my cousins was smoking a cigarette, a large machine gun resting in his lap, and a bandolier of bullets hanging from his chest. Claymore mines sat in a pile beside the jeep, along with tripwire and stocks of razor sharp bamboo. I held my M16 on my lap.

The village was one of the many Montagnard villages in the region, mostly from the Rahde tribe. Coffee plantations ran along the edge of a large river nearby. As breakfast came, many of the older men went to drink coffee under a tent.

I hopped out of the jeep and told Y-Alain to look after my weapon. I strolled toward the tent, the smell of fresh coffee filling the air. Three of the men in the tent were American. I had seen Americans other times, when they came to the village to talk with my father, but I had never seen a *soldier*. They wore green slacks and their heads were buzzed. They sat in the corner near the radio, which was playing music, though I couldn't recognize what they were singing about. The man they were calling "Lieutenant Briggs" stirred his coffee with a small wooden spoon, and brought the glass cup to his lips.

"What's the news, Lieutenant?" one of the Montagnards asked in French.

Briggs shook his head and rested the small cup on the arm of his chair. He had a silver striped bar on a patch sewed onto his green jacket. "Getting worse and worse. Had my men stationed out to defend a bridge."

"From Vietcong?"

"Don't care who they were," he said, painfully trying to smile. "We blew their heads off." He noticed I walked into the room, and paused before continuing. "We blocked off the whole bridge. They kept coming, we kept shooting."

"Ah," the Montagnard man nodded, understanding. "They don't give up."

"Sure don't," he sipped his coffee. "Couple of 'yards were there, they'll tell you."

"Briggs, Kowalski wants to talk to you—said it's urgent." one of the Americans said from the back room. He was holding a black box in his left hand, a black object in his right.

"Excuse me," Briggs said, walking to the back room.

It was nearing noontime as I exited the tent. I walked several feet to the nearest longhouse, walking up the steps made of tree trunks. The sky was a pale blue. White clouds rolled in. The sun seemed to drill into my flesh. Sweat rolled down my cheeks and as I stepped one foot into the entrance of the long-house, I heard a *woosh*, as if someone had swung a stick at my head and missed. A rush of heat washed over me. My ears rang—and I already knew what had happened before I turned and saw the tent I had just left replaced by a cloud of dust and fire.

"Artillery!" I heard from the back of the longhouse. The voice sounded muffled. I remember a man running out one of the rooms with his rifle in his hand. Another explosion sent me to my knees. He grabbed my wrist and lifted me up, dragging me from the longhouse.

"Go, go, to the bunker Y-Ben!" He shouted over the roar of crumbling houses and screams of the people. I didn't know who he was, but I wanted to show him I could shoot a gun—show him that I could kill as well as he could. But the way his eyes tore at mine forced me to the safety of the bunker a little ways behind the village. Several armed men led the trail of villagers to the fortress of concrete. I darted through the trees and brush and followed a villager into the bunker.

It was as small as the one near my home, but there were even more villagers than before. I sat down near the entrance. I remember thinking about my father, wondering if he was safe in Saigon—if the war there was as bad as it was here. I didn't feel safe behind the walls of the bunker. The vibrations of the artillery shook my spine and ribcage. I imagined the bunker collapsing from the artillery. Bodies crushed beneath the massive rubble of concrete and stone. Red gushing out from between the cracks.

I tried to force myself to forget about it. I heard another explosion followed by a scream from a man. He was wailing, "My leg!" I grew angry. I felt helpless. Seconds later, one more explosion—and his cry fell silent.

The artillery fell close to the bunker, but I did not move from the entrance. All the men with weaponry went to fight. I went too, with nothing but my hands and feet. No one pled with me to stay. They were as frantic, screaming and crying. Some were relatives, others were from different tribes. They all knew the dangers as much as I did.

I felt the ground tremble under my feet as I left. The burning huts filled my nostrils. I saw a man without his legs, lying in a pool of his own blood. I looked away, trying to suppress the puke that wanted to surface. I made my way back to the village. An American soldier ran beside me, confused. His eyes wandered over my face and the weapon I did not have. He didn't say a word, only slapped me on the shoulder and kept jogging forward.

The soldier started opening fire as soon as we hit the river. Trees surrounded the bank on each side. It was hard to make out anything on the other side of the embankment. I slid down the ridge and behind a mound of sandbags and a decaying log. The mud stuck to my trousers. I heard clacks of guns pierce the air.

"Hey!" A gruff voice shouted behind me. I turned to see Briggs running up to me, and then ducking behind cover. He popped open the top to his machine gun and handed me the ammo case. His cheek was black with dirt and soot—eyebrows singed off. "Help me with this!"

I stared at him awkwardly. I wanted to ask why he wasn't dead, but instead I opened the ammo case and fed it into the chamber. He closed the top, cocked the weapon and began spraying the trees.

I had to cover my ears. The weapon kicked back against his shoulder. Bullets whipped over my head and into the leaves and brush. Every time I saw a flash from the enemy's gun, Briggs would fire in that area and a body would roll down the bank and into the river.

The battle went on like this for half an hour. I continued to carefully feed the ammo, the string of bullets sliding over my hands. Briggs's rhythm had steadied into a constant burst fire. A few Americans took held the frontline, followed by four Montagnards. American sharpshooters sat in deep brush or thick trees, their bodies covered with a makeshift ghillie suit—a burlap poncho with wire holding leaves and branches together for camouflage. Briggs stopped firing. He squinted his eyes. I followed his gaze to a line of VC troops swarming the banks, crawling through the shallow river. The flashes on their AK-47s were blinding.

Briggs quickly lit a cigarette and slipped it between his lips as he started to fire. I watched a row of enemies fall before him. I felt a hand on my shoulder and Y-Alain and Y-Yôhan slid in next to me, ducking low and covering their heads.

"Here," Y-Alain handed me my rifle and quickly showed me how to work it. Aiming, firing, reloading. They opened up on the VC and I followed their lead. Adrenaline was pumping. I didn't know if my hands were shaking, or if it was the recoil of the gun between my palms. I fired, and saw a body drop into the river. I copied Y-Yôhan, firing disciplined bursts until I heard *clicks* when I hit the trigger. Reload. Fire away.

The river was a stream of blood. Men toppled from the bank on both sides of riverbed. We followed closely behind Briggs, moving where he moved, no more than two steps behind him.

The sun began to fall. The firing didn't cease. Briggs, Y-Yôhan, Y-Alain and I hunkered down behind a large sandbag barrier, peeking our heads over just to take shots. My shoulder drooped. My hands ached when I tried clenching them. I wanted to sleep. It felt as if I had run miles.

Briggs had emptied the last of his ammunition for his M60.

I offered my rifle. "You can use it better."

He shook his head and pushed the rifle against my chest, smiling. "Your weapon, soldier." He looked around and for the first time he pointed to the ground and said, "Stay here."

I watched him sprint behind a tree, bullets skewering trees beside him. He went into a crawl and inched his way forward to a dead soldier who had a belt of ammunition around his chest. Pulling it off, he ducked low behind a tree.

We fired at the other side of the river, hoping we could give him enough cover. We didn't. Briggs stepped from behind the trunk and broke out in a sprint. I remember a loud *crack*—louder than any other shot in the jungle. I remember Briggs's jaw, mangled and shredded. He stood in shock and reached for his chin but only found bits of flesh and blood. Another shot took the rest of his head off.

I held the M16 tight to my chest, unable to take my eyes off Briggs's limp body. The loud crack of the sharpshooter somewhere in the distance kept ringing in my ears like a church bell.

I realized we were alone, tired, and running low on ammunition. Most of the soldiers were higher up on the ridge with the exception of the Americans taking point. We were one of the only ones still this close to the river. I didn't want to move. My movements seemed robotic, fighting off of fear, firing my rifle into the brush. I didn't hit anything. I don't think I did. I was too tired to notice.

I ducked down to reload. I rose to fire and froze. Another swarm of VC troops rose up on our side. I saw Y-Alain firing more rapidly, his rhythmic fire becoming constant and erratic. They kept coming. The Americans became overwhelmed. Swarmed by the bayonets. I heard screams. *The end.* I thought. I closed my eyes and prayed.

A clap of thunder knocked me back. Flames showered upon the soldiers as American planes roared overhead. I hugged the ground. The explosions were so strong; they stirred my stomach and forced what little I had eaten into the dirt. Heat rushed over me. I managed to poke my head out the side of the sand-bags.

The other side of the river was engulfed in flames. The VC ran, the na-palm searing their flesh. Screams replaced their gunshots as they flailed wildly around the jungle and coffee plantations across the river. One of the Vietnam-ese soldiers tried to jump into the river. I could barely make out his body in the display of flames. The water splashed as the soldiers jumped in. They rose, the napalm sticking to their flesh—the fire ever present. Burning. The smell of charred flesh rose to my nostrils. There was nothing left in my stomach to puke out.

I had to cover my eyes. The flames were blinding. I rested against the sandbags, my legs unable to move under the exhaustion. The few VC troops left on our side were singled out by the sharpshooters out on the ridge.

"Come on, get up," Y-Yôhan muttered as he lifted me to my feet. I didn't check if the fire was spreading. I clung to his back, and he began to carry me up the ridge. He missed a step and we both fell on the mud, panting for air.

I wanted to fall asleep. But every time I closed my eyes I pictured Briggs with his jaw shot off. I go to Y-Yôhan who was sitting in a crouch, breathing heavily. I leaned on him for support as we inched up the slope to the village.

Splintered wood and bamboo littered the ground, along with bodies with missing limbs. French and Italian styled villas were crumbling mounds of stone and brick. Huts and longhouses were reduced to rubble and ash.

I collapsed, cross legged on the dirt and an American gave me a pail of water to drink from. I gulped it down. It had never tasted so sweet.

The fighting still went on a little deeper in the jungle. What was left of the village was safe. Napalm flickered over the mountains in the distance. They glowed red and orange.

Y-Yôhan, Y-Alain and I sat around the campire. The crackling flames licked at our shadows. Villagers threw what couldn't be saved into the fire. Scraps of the longhouses. Straw from huts. Wood from tattered merchant stands. Cries surrounded us as many lay loved ones to rest beneath the dirt.

I was squeezing my right hand, cramped and tense from holding the rifle so tightly. I thought of Briggs. I barely knew him, but I couldn't stop replaying his death in my head.

Y-Yôhan managed to sport a grin. He slapped my shoulder and said, "Guess God's looking out for us."

I looked at him. He was still smiling, but his eyes didn't match. They were focused on his necklace he was swinging back and forth next to the fire, the red and orange light casting a faint glow upon the gemstones.

"What do you mean?"

"I mean, we're not dead."

"How about all the other people?"

Y-Yôhan hesitated, and then shrugged. "Maybe it was their time."

I laid down on the dirt, resting my head on my hands. "I don't get it."

"It'll come eventually," he said.

"*Ama...*" Dad. I said the words softly. "He always said that killing was wrong."

"Yeah." He cleared his throat. "I mean—I don't know, maybe it's different, it doesn't make you or me bad people Y-Ben."

"Are you sure?"

Y-Yôhan smiled again and nodded. "Yeah, I'm sure. We kill to defend our homeland Y-Ben, don't forget that. They want to kill *every single one of us.* Because we worship God, because we're not *yuán.* God blessed us with these mountains—we have fight to hold onto what God has given us. Your *ama* also said these *yuán* will pay for their crimes in hell."

These yuán will go to hell? I thought. The storm clouds slowly rolled over the sky and began devouring the stars. The moon disappeared, and all I could see was the embers of the dying fire. *We kill them, they kill us—in the end, aren't we all wrong?*

I tried understanding. Maybe if I did, Y-Yôhan would think I was grown up. But I could only nod and pretend. It didn't make sense, and but I tried convincing myself that we were the right side—where we could kill without remorse. At the same time, I knew what the *yuán* did. Using children as human shields. Recruiting other Montagnards into their ranks to fight against their own people. Torture and imprisonment. I realized I hated them. I realized I wanted to kill every single one of them.

Y-Yôhan repeated, "I'll come eventually. Don't think too hard."

"OK," was all I could say as he helped me to my feet. My weak knees began to buckle, but he helped me stay up. I didn't object when he picked me up on his back and carried me back to one of the few standing longhouses, where many villagers had crowded into. Some built makeshift shelters of scrap metal and wood, straw and bamboo. Fiery lamps emitted a sweet aroma that floated over what was left of this village. My mother always said they were to ward off the insects. Dad would say they were a fire hazard, but wouldn't object.

We passed by the graves of the fallen heroes. They would never be recognized. Never be given a medal to show their bravery and undying love for their homeland.

My eyes began to droop after the first drops of rain fell on my cheek, wiping the dirt away. I remember Y-Yôhan staring out into the decimated village before entering the house. I wondered what he was thinking. Maybe he was remembering. Soccer games. Stick fighting before supper. Trying to train monkeys.

Those were the fondest memories of our childhood. With each body that floated down the river. Each man or woman we buried in the dirt and dust, it felt lost. All we could think of was guns, ash, and blood. All we saw was the explosions that rippled in the distance. All we heard was the monsoon rain pounding against sheet of scrap metal.

And all we knew was that we had to fight.

6

During the war, Americans had a saying. Boys become men when they turn eighteen and sign up for the draft, when they will fight for their country—for their freedom.

My son and I sat in a crowded Starbucks at the mall. I asked him what he planned to do after high-school, and he was quiet. "So?" I pressed.

"I was thinking the military. I like action, adventure, stuff like that. Besides, a lot of my friends are joining." He paused when he saw the worried look on my face. "A recruiter came to our school, he was telling us about it."

I finished my coffee and then took a deep breath. "There's a lot he left out."

August 8, 1973

My mother would always make the best fish for my birthday. I know my father always drooled over her cooking. I'd never eat it all. I fed what scraps were on my plate to the dogs. The whole village would celebrate, and I'd sleep well, knowing that tomorrow I could go out into the marketplace at the heart of Buôn Ma Thuột City and spend the birthday money. But I couldn't sleep tonight. My birthday.

The rain wouldn't stop. Through the small slit in the tent I could see lightning flash across the sky, and hear distant rumbles in the distance. I rolled over and closed my eyes, trying to sleep.

My mind ran through memories. I was recruited into MIKE Force three months earlier, a special branch of the United States Special Forces that focused on training the "indigenous soldier." That meant us Montagnards. We knew the land the best, the in-and-outs of the highlands.

I served in a squad of twelve—eleven Montagnards with our squad leader Sergeant Eric Kowalski leading the reconnaissance missions. That was our only task so far—reconnaissance. I didn't think today was going to be different.

I woke up to Y-Yôhan slipping his boots on. The two other soldiers in our tent were already gone. I sat up and slipped my trousers on. I wasn't wearing any underwear. Crotch rot was a bad problem. Constantly wading in cold water would cause the blood to leave that area, and eventually it would lead to fungus or even rotting, occurring mostly to the feet.

"Another recon assignment," Y-Yôhan said. He blew a jet of cigarette smoke from his nostrils. Bags drooped from his eyes, and a jagged scar now ran clear from his chin to his right ear. In a few short years, his body had been sculpted into that of a warrior.

I nodded. I was two inches shorter than Y-Yôhan, but now I had thirty pounds over him. I had three puckered scars left from a firefight; one in each shoulder and another in my gut. When Kowalski found out about it, he called me Y-Brick. "Bricks are tough to crack", he'd say.

We were constantly exhausted. No matter how hard we fought; no matter how many people we killed and no matter how many of our brothers would die—it always seemed like we were losing. And if we weren't fighting, we didn't sleep. We couldn't.

A chopper was there at exactly 0600 hours. Its side was scarred with machine gun fire. The Americans gave every helicopter with this model the name "Huey". We had done reconnaissance missions like this time and time again. It started becoming routine.

We boarded the Huey and a few minutes later we were high above the mountains. They looked different from the leafy green jungles of my childhood, and the clear water that ran through the highlands. My home was gone. The jungles were reduced to dirt and clay patches, burned to the roots from spilled napalm. Trash, debris, and bodies floated down the rivers.

I was staring aimlessly out the window of the chopper as we glided across a jagged mountain top. My equipment jangled against my leg as the propellers shook the aircraft. The inside smelled like urine and gasoline.

"Approaching the LZ," the pilot shouted from the cockpit. Everyone grabbed their guns. Checked their equipment.

"Ready?" Y-Yôhan asked. He was juggling his necklace in his palm. I noticed it was a nervous habit of his.

"Yeah."

"You've been quiet."

"I know." I spotted a fume of black smoke rising from the mountains.

"She's with God now."

I nodded, my eyes never leaving the burning jungle. My father and Y-Alain had sent the word from Buôn Ma Thuột that my mother had been caught in an artillery strike. I remember hearing my father's throat tightening as he shouted through the phone. He said there was nothing left of her. He said kill those Vietnamese dogs.

I felt a hand on my shoulder. I looked up into Kowalski's hardened, hazel eyes. He had a fresh cigarette between his lips, and was always grinning. "Don't be mopin' Y-Brick," he said.

I didn't exactly know what "moping" meant, but I could guess. Serving with the Americans for the last couple of years had rubbed off—I could understand most Basic English, a lot of military terms, and especially the profanities that arose almost every other word. "Yes, sir," I said, attempting my best English. He howled with laughter.

The chopper touched down in the middle of a clearing. We jumped off, one by one onto the marsh grass, flattened by the chopper's rotor wash. The chopper hovered low, swaying. The pilot kept his hand steady. We tossed our packs down first, and then jumped. Too many soldiers came back with broken bones when they jumped with their heavy packs. Our boots sank instantly in the thick mud. The strong winds shook trees as it took off, leaving us in the foggy morning of the jungle. Dark clouds were rolling in fast from the east— we had to act quickly before the rain fell. Once it came, it wouldn't stop for weeks, months even.

We hadn't been engaged in any fighting yet. We walked silently, some of the guys muttering about not being able to see their girlfriends back home, or eating a home cooked meal. I only cared about getting out alive.

I took point with Y-Yôhan and Kowalski. We were almost silent. Our eyes kept alert, scanning the jungle floor. Birds squawked loudly above us, followed by monkeys, who seemed to screech every time we set a foot down on the grass. I was looking for any sign of activity, or traps—broken twigs, cleared brush and bamboo, tripwire, bundles of leaves stacked on top of tiger pits. I remember watching one of my squad members fall into a tiger pit, the nearly invisible wire mesh coated with leaves giving way. Punji sticks, or sharpened bamboo stakes, were sticking out at the bottom. The man was dead before he got a chance to scream.

Kowalski had tossed his cigarette in a nearby stream. He didn't want the smell to drift anywhere. He was one of the more fearless squad leaders. Fearless, not reckless. He was smart, intimidating, but fatalistic. "Won't stop 'till I'm dead," he'd always say.

We had been walking cautiously for thirty minutes before we encountered a small shoulder of a road. Kowalski signaled the group to halt and Y-

Yôhan and I snuck into a crouch. As we heard voices, our crouch flattened out to a prone and we began to crawl over the shoulder. I peeked over first and my heart stopped.

They were no more than twenty feet from me. Hundreds of them, NVA regulars dressed in green fatigues and helmets that seemed to cover their eyes. Polished AK-47's hung from their shoulders. They helped haul boxes down the trail that seemed to curve around our position. Some were stashed in crates, probably infantry ammunition. Larger pieces were carried individually—mortars especially. I didn't have to look up to see soldiers hidden in trees on top of a large hill guarding the other side of the road. It was a perfect trail for a supply line—hidden deep in the jungle and surrounded on both sides.

It didn't make sense. The NVA usually slept during the day and worked at night. In our past missions, we had taken the coordinates of the area while the NVA was sleeping, and at night, the bombers would come in. This situation changed everything.

I made hand signals back at Kowalski, telling him to move up prone. He did so, and when he reached the shoulder, he took a look for himself. He quickly ducked back down, swearing under his breath.

"We're surrounded." Kowalski bit his lip. We had never been so close to a supply column before.

We moved a little further back from the shoulder, out of sight, in the prone. I could only assume we were lucky they didn't see us when we were walking around like idiots earlier.

Kowalski swore silently through gritted teeth and pulled out his radio. He whispered the coordinates. I understood. If they NVA were working now, they were probably almost through their trail of supplies. Calling in the gunship now would be the only way to get the job done.

For the first time during a mission, my ears were hot, and my heart was racing. I tried to clear the lump in my throat, but I didn't want to make any noise. I could hear some of the soldiers behind me breathing. I wanted to tell them to shut up. Y-Yôhan signaled the men in the rear to stay alert, and I let them know we were surrounded. No one moved.

"No, no, not yet," Kowalski whispered and readjusted the receiver to his ear. "We're too close; give us five mins to clear out."

Kowalski tucked the receiver in its box and looked back at us. "We got five minutes before they blow this place to kingdom come."

We began crawling, sliding through the mud on our bellies. I remember thinking what would happen if they saw us. I imagined an ambush from the trees. Bullets raining from behind, tearing through our bodies. We'd be trapped between their jaws like mice. "Drop your weapons", they would say. They'd order us on our knees, and execute us one by one like animals.

A lucky break. The snipers on the hilltop didn't seem to notice. I heard Vietnamese voices no more than ten feet to my right, a wall of brush and bamboo separating us. We began to backtrack toward the LZ. Our crawl turned into a low crouch as the voices began to fade in the distance. Soon we were sprinting, our boots sloshing through the mud. We heard a loud *bzzt bzzt* followed by rumbles in the distance. The gunship was taking down the supply column.

"My God, ain't that a beautiful sound." Kowalski stopped moving and grinned. The gunship was nicknamed "Puff the Magic Dragon".

I gave him a blank stare and tried to catch my breath, muttering, "Easy."

"Bravo One this is Recon Team, requesting dust-off. Over," Kowalski said.

"Roger that Recon, ETA two min—"

There was a pause, and followed by swearing over the other end. The radio began to break up. "What's goin' on? Over." Silence.

We stood there, motionless. Kowalski took a long drag on his cigarette until there was nothing left but the butt. He tossed it in the marsh with a shaking hand and looked over his shoulder as a loud roar came over the trees. We all heard it.

Bravo One's chopper was spinning like a top. Its hull had been shredded—the engine was a fiery display of red and orange with black fumes leaking from the bottom. The rear propeller was completely torn off. A stream of tracer fire followed the chopper. It seemed to happen so slowly. The bullets pierced the cockpit. I saw blood spew onto the shattered windows. The bird disappeared over the trees and we heard a crash in the jungle.

Kowalski bit his lip and spat curses. His knuckles seemed to glow white from gripping his weapon so tightly. "Move out."

We followed closely. It wasn't easy losing soldiers. Kowalski had talked highly of Bravo One. He said they were his brothers. The best pilots the army had. Kowalski broke out in full stride, leaping over logs and upturned roots. He muttered under his breath, something about "not letting those gooks near the bird".

"What do you think?" I asked Y-Yôhan when I caught up to him.

"They're dead," he said, shaking his head. "No way they're still alive after that. You saw what happened." He cleared his throat and began to slow down. "He's in shock."

"There's nowhere else to go—that was our evac," I said.

"Anywhere is better than here—you don't think the *yuán* are on their way too?" He asked. I nodded and flicked the safety off my rifle.

The helicopter had crashed between two large trees. The murky swamp water had extinguished the fire before the chopper exploded. The main propeller was completely trashed, ripped apart by the thick bark of the trees. Kowalski approached recklessly, leaping up onto the nose of the chopper and examining the pilot and co-pilot, both who were lying in pools of their own blood. The pilot's face was indistinguishable, bits of brain spilling out over the shattered skull. The other pilot had been shot straight through the neck.

I didn't know what to expect from Kowalski. I thought he was about to pull his rifle and go hunting for the Vietnamese. Maybe swear until he was out of breath. "Get into position."

Won't stop till he's dead.

I wished there was a mounted M60 on the chopper. Maybe we could've saved more lives that day. The *yuán* were coming from the east. We could hear their shouts. Four men took the chopper for cover. Five guarded the flanks, and had already wired claymore mines along the perimeter. Kowalski, Y-Yôhan and I took the lead defensive position at the east.

We waited. Thunder rumbled above us. Rain began to clash against the swampy waters. I spotted a leech burying itself in Y-Yôhan's calf. I blinked, and the Vietnamese troops moved in. They were moving slowly, cautious and alert. Taking point was a soldier wielding a large machine gun. They kept coming. In the rain, it was hard to make out, but not for Kowalski.

"Gotta be at least twenty or more," he whispered, just barely over the rain. "Wait 'till I give the signal."

I took in long breaths, hands around my weapon. Finger resting on the trigger. The Vietnamese soldiers seemed to be sure there were no survivors. Then it began.

The machine gunner stepped on a claymore's tripwire. He was tossed against a tree, his body blown in half. The man next to him also took the impact of the blast, the steel balls concealed in the claymore shredding his body. The rest began to shout, shouldering their weapons. We spun from behind the trees and fired, dropping three more before they got to cover.

It was a stalemate for a few minutes. Two sides fired aimlessly, bullets skimming over the swamp water. It couldn't have been even noon yet, but the rain clouds gave us darkness. I found one soldier crawling in the water on his elbows and knees. I saw a grenade explode next to him, the muddy water splashing red.

I remember Kowalski screaming, "cover that flank!" and then running over to the north flank across the open field. Both our soldiers guarding that flank were dead. The NVA took aim at Kowalski, and I think we were all surprised that he wasn't shot dead. I fired from behind a tree, unable to see if I was even hitting anything.

Y-Yôhan yelped as he hit the ground, clutching his chest. I thought he died. The bullet went in one shoulder and out the other. I slid in beside him.

"I can't breathe," he said.

"Hang in there, you're fine," I wanted to smile. The same place I had been shot years before. "Don't be a wuss." I propped Y-Yôhan up against the cover of a tree and told him to stay put, running back up to the frontline.

The Vietnamese forces were thinning out. We began to push forward. I heard them shouting "retreat". Kowalski didn't allow it. My M16 jammed. I drew the .45 from my hip and began to fire, picking my shots carefully. There was one soldier left, taking pot shots at us from behind a fallen log. He was using a rifle with a large scope mounted at the top. Two more of our men fell to his well-placed shots.

I gripped the pin of my grenade tightly, but Kowalski came over and slapped my hand. He said, "Come with me," and we crouched behind trees, moving slowly toward the log. What was left of our squad fired on the soldier, making sure he was never able to peek up. We closed in, pushing ourselves against the sand bags. We were separated by inches. Our squad stopped firing.

I was hoping there was only one on the other side. An image of two, even three soldiers crossed my mind. Throwing a grenade would be the most logical option. But as I watched Kowalski draw his serrated combat knife, I knew it wasn't an option at all.

The soldier slung his weapon over, shouldered. Kowalski lunged, batting the weapon aside just as it went off and dove over the sandbags. I rose and found another soldier in the back, trying to get a steady shot at Kowalski, who was slashing frantically at the man beneath him. I fired three bullets, the last finding the soldier's head.

Kowalski was clearly larger than the NVA regular. He shoved his knife into the man's throat and then twisted it. The man made a sickening gurgle noise as eyes rolled to the back of his head. Kowalski yanked the blade to one side, blood mixing in with the rain

He stood up and kicked the corpse's head, which was dangling by a thread of skin. I didn't know what to say. I didn't know what I thought of him at this point. Fearless and smart seemed like a cover-up for cruel and efficient. He put his knife in its scabbard and looked at me.

I don't know what he saw in my eyes, but he lowered his head and said bitterly, "Go get Y-Yôhan, we're gettin' outta this jungle."

Y-Yôhan was still clutching his shoulder as I approached. He moaned as I helped him to his feet.

"Good, now you're a soldier," Kowalski said. He put on a boonie hat and lit another cigarette. "Get up. We need to move."

There were only six of us left. Kowalski stripped the bodies of their dogtags and ammunition. He placed the dogtags in my hand.

"You're good men. Off-record, I'd rather have you fighting with me than some of these privates back at base," he smiled, and then added, "You should see'em, couldn't hit a tree in this jungle if they wanted to."

"We just want to keep our land," I managed.

Kowalski took a drag on his cigarette and nodded. We began to make our way through the swampy waters and the rain. Y-Yôhan winced with each step. Kowalski told us we had to get clear because the LZ was too hot. I tucked the dogtags in my pocket and continued through a bamboo wall. Leeches clung to my calves, but I didn't care, I was alive.

We were wading through the water, waist deep, rifles above our heads, when Kowalski looked at me and grinned. His eyes were solemn. "Heck of a birthday, aye?"

7

It was already dark outside. My son was sick in bed. I was watching a documentary on the History Channel, something about soldiers in the Vietnam War, how they survived for days out in the jungle.

They couldn't tell me anything I didn't already know, so I got up and walked into my son's room. He was fiddling with his laptop.

"Shouldn't you be resting?"

"I just woke up," he said. "What're you watching?" he called out.

"Documentary on the History Channel."

"Leave it on. I'm getting up."

I went and sat at the foot of his bed. "I'll sum it up for you."

August 9, 1973

I sat with my father on the edge of a small fishing boat. The water was so clear I could see the clouds in them. Trees surrounded us on both sides, their trunks arching in the mountain wind. I held a small bamboo fishing pole in my hands. I waited for a bite.

My father's eyes seemed hollow as he stared out over the edge of the mountains. His face was worn and ragged. A thick beard flowed over his chin. He was balding.

"When will it stop?" I heard myself ask. My voice sounded distant, as if I hadn't really said anything.

"When God wants it to." His line twitched. A fish took the bait. He didn't move.

I wanted to reach out and drag the fish in for him, but I didn't. He watched the line then looked back up at the clouds.

"*Ama*," I said. Father.

"Hm?"

I wanted to ask him so many things. I wanted to ask how he felt when mom died. I wanted to see if he was still alive inside. But I knew he wouldn't answer. "Never mind," I surrendered reluctantly. I followed his gaze to the horizon. There was nothing there but a blue sky cut off by rounded mountain tops. I leaned back in the boat and closed my eyes. The sun was soft and warm against my skin. *This is nice.*

———

"Get up," I heard. I sat up and looked around. I couldn't see a thing in the darkness. I had been resting against an upturned root on top of a thick pile of mud. Cold water dripped from the trees.

"It's Nhean," the voice said. Nhean was one of the Cambodians in our squad. He specialized in arming and disarming explosives. He was fluent in our native tongue. "Kowalski says we're moving out."

"I'm just happy he let us sleep," I muttered, feeling around for my weapon. It was leaning against a tree, my pack lying underneath it to keep it out of the mud. Our rifles had a tendency to jam at the worst times. My eyes were starting to adjust. I could see vague silhouettes of trees. The ground sometimes flickered with light, as the pale moon reflected off the muddy water.

"I think he needed some rest after that." Nhean sloshed around in the mud.

"We all needed some rest after that," I corrected. We were only a couple of miles from Bravo One's crash site. The region was crawling with NVA troops. We called for an evac twice, but that was a no-go. The clouds were too thick. The fog was too thick. NVA machine-gunners spotted in the area. Once our radio malfunctioned, we thought we were toast. We were blind in the bush.

Kowalski was spinning his .44 Magnum around his fingers as I approached. Y-Yôhan was smoking a cigarette. Two of the other soldiers stood next to them. I didn't know much about them, except that they were Laotian and could only understand a few words in Montagnard and English.

"Clouds rollin' in," Kowalski muttered. "Fog's thick. No evac today either."

"We should keep going," Y-Yôhan said. He was rotating his shoulder, the bullet wound obviously irritating him.

Kowalski slung his rifle over his shoulder and grabbed a compass from his jacket pocket. The needle spun to the north. "Closest firebase was about thirty miles northeast from our insertion."

"So we're going to walk through miles of jungle, swarming with NVA, claymores, tiger pits and whatever else they have out there?" Nhean asked.

Kowalski growled at Nhean. He stood almost a head taller than Nhean, and was almost twice as large. "Questioning my orders?"

"No." Nhean looked away from his eyes.

"Then shut up," Kowalski snarled. He tucked his .44 into its holster. "Let's try to cover some ground before Charlie pops out of the bushes and yell surprise."

———

It was getting colder. The loud buzzing of crickets and the hymn of birds pierced the air. It took quite a bit of effort to trudge through the thick mud. Eventually, the water got so deep we had to hold our rifles above our heads. When we got through the river, Kowalski lit a cigarette, took a drag and then pressed the burning end against a leech that had found his calf. We checked each other, spraying the leeches off with a bottle of insect repellent. The little things hated it. One spray and they'd curl up and fall off, inching their way back to the water.

Nhean was lagging behind. Kowalski nudged my arm with the butt of his rifle and said, "Hey, check on that guy, would ya?"

I groaned and walked to the back of the column. Nhean was walking slowly, and I noticed a limp in his step. His face was strained. "Hey, what's the deal?"

"Nothing," he muttered.

"You're holding us up," I said.

"Well I'll just sit back here and rot, is that better?" Nhean asked.

"That'd be lovely," Y-Yôhan chuckled from the front.

"Wait," I told the rest of the group. The men groaned and sat down against the trees to catch their breath.

Kowalski was pissed. "What's goin' on?" he asked, marching over.

"Take off your boots, Nhean," I said, trying not to raise my voice.

"No." He shifted uneasily, his eyes on the ground.

Kowalski understood. "Take off your boots or I'll hack'em off." He pulled his knife from his hip. The serrated edge was still bloody.

Nhean flinched. "Alright, alright." He struggled to pull off his boots, cringing at the motion. He managed to get one boot and sock off. I grimaced when I saw his foot. It was swollen and was discolored. Pus oozed out from the open sores. One of the Laotian soldiers decided to check his feet as well, paranoid of the jungle rot.

Kowalski shook his head. "We gotta get a medevac, pronto."

"How long has it been like that?" I asked.

"I don't care," Kowalski said. "That thing's gonna gangrene, if we don't get a medevac soon."

"I'll stay here, then," Nhean said.

"And become a tiger's chew toy? I don't think so," Kowalski said. He pulled Nhean to his feet. "Get up. We'll carry you if we have to." We all groaned. "Quit complaining. This ain't daycare."

Nhean pulled his sock and boot over his foot and struggle to stand. I let him lean on me, and we fell in behind the rest.

"Should've told us sooner," I said.

"What good would that have done?"

I didn't say anything. There was nothing we could do about it now, not even a dose of morphine to ease the pain. We usually had a corpsman, a medical marine, traveling with the squad. Most of us knew herbal remedies—or "voodoo" as Kowalski called it—but we knew nothing of gangrene.

I sighed. "Get on my back," I said, crouching down.

"What?"

"Just do it, or I'll let you crawl."

"Fine." He hopped on my back. He was light, but the combined weight of him and his pack was exhausting.

I caught up with the rest of the squad. They didn't say anything, but from the looks on their faces, they were clearly relieved that someone else had to carry Nhean. It wasn't in my nature to leave people behind. I don't think it was in Y-Yôhan's nature either.

"Can't you go any faster?" Nhean joked.

"I swear, I'll dump you right here," I shot back.

Suddenly, we froze. I slowly set Nhean down, who wobbly stood before crouching to balance himself. It was Y-Yôhan. He was in front of Kowalski, holding a palm up. He had spotted something.

We weren't traveling on a trail, where most of traps were sprung, but we always had to be alert. Y-Yôhan was exceptional at this. I saw it too, seconds later, thin wire gleaming in the moonlight. The tripwire could've been for several different things. Claymore mines were the most feared. I remember a soldier telling me that the NVA and VC were sticking punji sticks into mudballs and using them as pendulums that swung down when a wire was tripped. Never saw them myself, but I didn't doubt it.

"What is it?" I whispered. If there was a trap, there could be a patrol nearby.

"Claymore mines," Y-Yôhan said.

"I'll get it," Nhean said. We took a few steps back and let Nhean walk over to the tripwire. He stood still, following the tripwire to a claymore, and then followed that tripwire to small nest to the side. He warned us, and we backed up even more.

"This is going to be tricky," he said. "They're daisy chained." Daisy chained meant the claymores were wired to each other. If one exploded, then all of them would.

"We could pass by it," Y-Yôhan suggested.

"So the next patrol can get blown to pieces?" Kowalski asked.

"If he messes up, we're dead," I stated. "NVA will flock here in seconds."

"I won't let anymore men get carried out in their ponchos," Kowalski said. "Now get those mines outta' here."

"This doesn't feel right," I managed, adding in, "sir."

"Of course it doesn't. Nothing feels right in this god forsaken jungle," Kowalski said.

I watched Nhean tinker with the side of the claymore. I heard a *snip* and then he looked back at us, flashing a thumbs-up. "Main mine is down, the others are out in the open."

"Get them too," Kowalski said.

"Alright, *boss*." Nhean sighed and began to hobble over to the nest of mines. He ducked down for a couple of seconds and swore. I heard a click. We dove backwards and covered our heads. An explosion rippled through the ground. My ears rang. Dirt and mud rained over our bodies. Instinctively, I reached for my weapon and found cover behind a large tree. Silence.

I saw Kowalski creep up from behind a log and stare across the marsh. He made a hand motion. No enemies sighted. I crawled over to him and Y-Yôhan.

"I think Nhean tripped the nest," Y-Yôhan said.

"Ya' think?" Kowalski asked.

"Could've been remote," I suggested. I didn't hear anything but our heavy breathing.

"Doesn't matter,," Kowalski said. "NVA are probably on their way. Let's go." We carefully walked over the ground the claymores had just unearthed.

We couldn't find any trace of Nhean except for a leg, an arm, and his rifle, blown a few yards down the path. The rifle was damaged badly, but I was able to salvage the magazine.

I took point with Y-Yôhan. Our jog turned into a sprint as we spotted flashlights behind us. Branches whipped past my face, and brush scratched my arms as we darted through them. And then—a thick bamboo patch.

We took a detour to the east, hugging the bamboo wall and staying low. The flashlights started to get closer. I knew we couldn't risk a firefight and get cornered against the bamboo patch. We'd be overwhelmed in seconds. We were already low on ammunition. Voices drew nearer, but we caught a lucky break and found a small nook in the bamboo wall. It was barely visible, hidden by thick brush and swaying leaves. Kowalski ducked in and pulled us through one by one. It was cramped, but we managed to fit while all lying flat in the mud. It reeked.

"Anything?" I heard a voice shout in Vietnamese. "No", was the response. "Keep looking."

I held my breath. I felt like breathing was too loud. They'd hear me and tear up the bamboo with their rifles until we were mangled pieces of flesh. We didn't move. I didn't dare shift my head to look behind me. Footsteps grew louder. Mud sloshed and churned. I saw a flashlight on the ground in front of me. Then, a soldier's boot.

"Nothing," the soldier said. He looked behind him. Then slowly, he moved away. The footsteps and voices disappeared. Darkness.

After a couple of minutes, Y-Yôhan emerged from the brush and looked around. Nothing. He gave us the "OK" to step out. The NVA had disappeared into the fog. It didn't take us long to realize we had been lying in a pile of manure.

"Not how I planned for my stay in the bush," Kowalski said, wiping his hands on his already stained trousers. "Gah."

The Laotians laughed. I couldn't help from smiling when Y-Yôhan went and hugged Kowalski. We all looked ridiculous, breathing heavily, our sweat mixing in with the muck that clung to our fatigues.

When the sun began to rise, we had traveled a couple more miles toward the fire base. I was thinking of Nhean, wondering if he had any family back home. Wondering if he had a girl, waiting for his reply to her letter. It troubled me that we couldn't go back and search for his body. The NVA would undoubtedly double the patrols around that area. It would be a suicide mission.

A village appeared in the distance. The fog had cleared, and the storm clouds seemed to skip right over us. The sun was out, beating against our faces as we walked closer. We stopped on the edge of a small hill, where Kowalski looked through his binoculars.

"Can't tell," he said.

Y-Yôhan paused and looked through the sights. "Montagnard."

"Positive?" Kowalski asked.

"Yes."

I used my hand to block the sun and looked up. Sky was clear. "We need a radio."

"Think they have one?" Kowalski asked.

Y-Yôhan shrugged.

"Well let's find out." Kowalski began to move down the hill toward the village. We followed after him.

The villagers greeted us kindly, offering food and rice wine. We took them generously, but Y-Yôhan and I knew that they didn't have much to spare. We took small portions, and Kowalski reluctantly agreed to do the same. We sat down in one of the longhouses around a circular table with two men. One of them was the Chieftain.

"Do you have a radio?" I asked the Chieftain. He was old, his head balding and his skin wrinkled. But he talked normal and sat tall.

"Radio…" he paused in thought. "You mean, music?"

"No, no, like—"

"Oh, military radio?"

"Yes."

"No," he said. "Americans were here a couple of hours ago; they went back up on the trail."

I told Kowalski.

"Ask him how many," he said.

I did, and the Chieftain shrugged. "Twenty? Maybe thirty…"

"Jesus." Kowalski sat back. "Must've been a whole platoon."

"We might be able to track them," Y-Yôhan said. "They might be moving slow with all the men."

Kowalski nodded and stood up to shake the man's hand. "Thank you for the food."

Nightfall. We traveled through the trees beside the road. We hadn't caught a glimpse of the platoon. Sure enough, there were footprints all over the trail, but until we spotted them, we couldn't take the risk of taking the main road.

"I'm starting to think they had more than a couple of hour's head start." Kowalski stepped over a fallen log.

"Hey, you're the one that's supposed to be telling us not to complain." I said so Kowalski couldn't hear. Y-Yôhan laughed.

"What's so funny princess?" Kowalski asked.

"Nothing," Y-Yôhan said.

Kowalski grunted.

We heard a shout up ahead. I couldn't make it out, but I got excited. It wasn't in Vietnamese. Kowalski led us forward. We kept along the side of the trail, as quiet as possible. I saw them, a line of twenty to thirty marines, walking single file. Even with a group that large, they were prone to an ambush. It wasn't smart.

"Stay low," Kowalski said. "Don't know if they have any trigger-happy marines, but it's not worth the risk of finding out." Kowalski stopped on the sloping shoulder beside the road and shouted from the shadows. "What company?"

The marines froze. One shakily answered back, "Charlie."

"This is Sergeant Kowalski, I'm coming out." He stepped out of the brush. We followed behind. Some of the marines looked confusingly at us.

"Who're they?"

"Them mountain men."

"Whaddya call'em? 'Yards?'"

"That's right."

The marine who appeared to be in charge walked up to Kowalski. He was tall and wore thick, round glasses. "Jesus, Sarge, you scared the crap out of us. Lance Corporal Anderson. We've been going blind for days now—no radio, no nothin'."

"You too?" Kowalski asked. "We've been traveling without a radio for twenty, thirty miles." Kowalski shook his head. "You in charge?"

"No, sir, Second Lieutenant Adams is coors."

"Coors?" I asked Y-Yôhan.

"KIA," he said. "Dead."

Kowalski frowned. "What's your assignment?"

"A firebase down the trail was gettin' hammered by shells, so they wanted us to blow the crap out of an NVA ammo dump," Anderson said, nervously adjusting his glasses. "It was an ambush."

"There's a firebase not too far from here. Can I ask why you think it was a good idea to take the trail?" Kowalski asked.

"I—I don't know, sir," Anderson stuttered.

"Everyone fall in behind me." Kowalski lit a cigarette. "And stay off the trail unless you want your brains blown out."

We filed in behind Kowalski. He always said he never wanted to lead a platoon. Too many "crybabies" to take care of. Most platoon leaders were boot lieutenants, straight from an academy. They were inexperienced, but smart. Kowalski said smarts didn't matter much in the bush. *You gotta know how to shoot, and shoot fast.*

"I thought the Americans were smart enough to stay off the trail," I said, grinning. "They could take a lesson from us."

"We're not even a part of their army, though." Y-Yôhan took a puff from his cig. "We're replaceable."

"Not to Kowalski," I said. "He doesn't have a problem with us."

"Of course not," he said. "But to the rest of them, we're just another dumb pair of rice

eating gooks."

We kept walking. Kowalski spat a string of curses words at any marine who dared complain. We took point with him. He was grinning, as usual, with a cigarette between his lips. He was the only American who depended on us— trusted us. He wasn't like the rest.

"He *needs* us," Y-Yôhan whispered, reading my thoughts.

The jungle was still. The only thing I could hear was the mud beneath our boots and the constant chatter between the marines. I gave a short prayer, asking for safety. I found myself asking when everything would return to normal. Then I realized maybe I didn't know what normal was.

8

The flashes of red and blue awoke me from my sleep, followed by a hard knock at the front door. I rolled over in bed and told my wife I'd get it.

She watched tiredly from the bed as I pulled on my sweatpants and left our bedroom. I turned on the lights in the living room and cracked the front door.

My son stood, eyes lowered to the "welcome home" rug beneath his feet, with a pudgy police officer standing behind him.

I furrowed my brows and looked at this officer. I didn't know what to say.

"We found him running from a party," the officer finally grunted. "Gave us quite the chase."

"I didn't do anything," my son said, "I was just there with some friends." He didn't look up.

"Thank you, officer," I said. "I'll take care of this."

I sat my son down at the dinner table and brewed a pot of coffee. My wife walked in, and I gave her a look that said, "Honey, I can handle this."

"I didn't do anything," my son repeated.

"I believe you," I said, reading the look of surprise on his face. I listened to the rumble of the coffee machine and took in the aroma. "I raised you better."

April 4, 1975

From the window of the Huey, Saigon looked like a different world. It was bustling with activity. Cars inched forward through pedestrian-filled streets. Large ships drifted in and out of the harbor. The city seemed to stretch for miles. Several helicopters floated in and out of the city, lifting refugees and evacuating civilians. The NVA was getting closer. Was only a matter of time.

We had spent the past few months away from combat. Our reconnaissance missions became routine. Kowalski left for R&R a few days ago, just before we got the call from Bravo to report to headquarters. We had been operating from a small village on the outskirts of Buôn Ma Thuột, which had been overrun by Vietnamese forces a few months back. Bravo sent choppers to transfer our company to a base near Saigon.

There were some new members in our squad. The two Laotians had survived, and Kowalski left Y-Yôhan and I in charge of the squad while he was gone. "Can't wait to see my baby," he kept saying. The newest member was a Laotian named Keon. He joined the squad three months ago, having been recommended to Kowalski from another Lieutenant who said, "he fights well." He was about a year younger than I was, but he was skinnier and in my eyes, he didn't look like a soldier at all.

The base was only about two or three miles away on the outskirts of Saigon. It was walled off with gates of barbed wire and heavily fortified with neatly placed sandbags. Our chopper touched down on a small landing on base. There were a lot of marines nearby, loading supplies and ammunition to take to the frontlines into cargo birds. I stepped off and was immediately greeted by a man in worn fatigues and a green cap. His face was red. He didn't seem much older than I was. "Gunnery Sergeant Ross." He stuck out his hand.

"Y-Ben," I said, shaking his hand.

Y-Yôhan introduced himself.

"You're Kowalski's men, right?" Ross asked. "The 'yards?"

I nodded, as the rest of the squad filled in behind us.

Ross started to speak in our language. "Kowalski's got R&R? Lucky guy."

"He should be back in a week," Y-Yôhan said.

"Alright, we'll get you settled in." Ross began heading toward the barracks. "Kowalski didn't say anything about me?"

"Nope," I said.

Ross sighed, "I'm surprised. He's a good friend of mine, you know."

The barracks were constructed of long wooden boards, mesh screens for the windows, and a plethora of misguided nails. Soldiers were rapping on the wood with their hammers, the sound echoing across base. Tanks and jeeps rolled in, some scarred with bullets and shrapnel. Soldiers unloaded the wounded and the supplies.

"Looks like you guys might be here a while, at least until Kowalski gets back." Ross kicked a cot gently. "Might as well relax."

We began dropping our backpacks and weapons on the cots. Y-Yôhan and I took the ones nearest the door.

"Food's up the trail to the north. Heard they're serving steak today." Ross grinned. "I'll catch ya'll later." He left, the wooden door swinging shut in the muggy wind.

"Well, you heard him. Let's go eat," I said. *Steak. What a treat.*

The guys took off immediately, hollering cheerfully all the way to the cafeteria. I stopped in the doorway when I noticed Keon sitting cross-legged on one of the cots, lighting a cigarette. His hand was shaking.

"Coming?" I asked.

"Um, yeah," he responded. He blew a jet of smoke from his nose and coughed in his sleeve. "In a little bit. I'm kind of tired. Maybe I'll take a nap."

"OK, I'll save you a plate."

He nodded his thanks, and I made my way out of the barracks.

The cafeteria was a couple of makeshift tents, constructed of bamboo, wood and tarp to shield us from the sun. The Americans were grilling steaks. The scent of the meat floated through the air. Most of the seats were taken by the Americans already, so Y-Yôhan and our rest of the squad had to squat in the dirt next to the tables.

Y-Yôhan nodded his head to the grill. "Get some food."

I obliged, grabbing a plate off the table. The marine, serving steaks, looked me up and down, grinned, and said in a mocking tone, "Aw, mountain man want food?" He chuckled, and several of his buddies laughed with him. He stabbed a steak that hadn't been cooked yet and put it on my plate. "Here you go," he said. "Raw. Like you savages eat it."

I wanted to hit him, but instead, I stood there, patiently staring back. My brows furrowed.

He backed up a little. Thankfully, Ross stepped in. He pushed the marine so hard he hit the dirt.

"You're an idiot, you know that?" Ross said. He took the raw steak off my plate and put it on the marine's. He looked around at the men and said, "Anyone who wants to badmouth these 'yards—well, first I'll let them beat the crap out of you so bad you won't be able to tell night from day—then it'll be leeches for dinner. Everyone got that?"

"Yeah, Gunny," they groaned. The marine brushed himself off, and glared at me.

I smiled. "Thanks."

Ross shrugged. "I was doing the kid a favor. Come on, let's talk." He motioned to Y-Yôhan. "You too."

Y-Yôhan told the squad he'd be right back and tagged along with Ross and I. "What's up?"

"Just going to show you around the base," Ross said. "While we're at it, tell me about yourselves."

A man walked past me, hobbling on crutches. One of his legs was gone.

"We grew up in a village called Buôn Alê—near Buôn Ma Thuột," I explained. "Vietnamese attacked on Chinese New Year. Been fighting ever since."

Ross nodded and then pointed off in the distance. "Showers are that way—well, if you can call it that." Ross chuckled and then cleared his throat. "Well, tell me this—how do guys like you get in the Special Forces?"

"What do you mean, guys like us?" Y-Yôhan asked.

"You know, 'yards."

"MIKE Force," I said. We passed a makeshift hospital. Ross didn't have to point it out. The sight of bloodied soldiers, missing arms and legs, and doctors and nurses running around frantically was enough. Several tents were set up, where I could hear people screaming. Another small landing zone was set up behind the hospital, the roar of helicopters filling the air as more of the wounded were unloaded.

"I see," Ross said. "Training indigenous troops."

"Something like that," Y-Yôhan said. "Kowalski stayed behind like a few others."

"I'll tell ya what," Ross began, "It's a heck of a fine idea."

It felt like such a long time since I was recruited into MIKE Force. A couple of years had gone by in what seemed like minutes.

"Nothing else we could've done, really," Y-Yôhan said. "We'd be fighting either way."

"Might as well do it with better guns," I added.

Ross laughed.

"Got a point there." He lit a cigarette. He handed one to Y-Yôhan, and one to me, but I declined.

"Don't smoke?" he asked.

I remembered the burning jungle and the grey and black smoke rising from the tops of villages. I remembered soldiers flailing their arms, fire clinging to their bodies, the repulsive scent of burning flesh thick in the air. "Nah."

—————

"Drinks, here!" One of the Americans grabbed a can of beer and tossed it to another.

"How'd you manage to get all this?" another asked.

"You can thank the Gunny for that!" someone else blurted.

It was a cloudless night. I remembered Y-Yôhan handing me a beer. After that, it was a blur. Can after can. It was the first time I had ever been drunk, and it seemed like an eventful occasion at first.

"Old enough to kill, old enough to drink," Ross said, raising his can to mine, toasting the laughter of boys.

That's what we were—boys. And yet we were killing anything that moved. Killing anything that might kill us. It didn't matter if they were wearing black pajamas or green fatigues. It didn't matter if they were full-grown men with beards or children who would never experience their first kiss. They were the enemy. We had to kill them. We *had* to.

Ross, Y-Yôhan and I sat inside a large tent with a handful of marines, the ground littered with cans. Men would walk by, every now and then, saying, "Thanks for the rations Gunny," in a sarcastic tone. Ross and Y-Yôhan walked outside to find more beer, and Keon staggered up to me, a can in his hand. He sat down next to me and learned his head against the side of a wooden chair.

"What's up Keon!" I shouted, smacking him on the chest with a limp fist.

He shrugged. "I'm tired."

"Aw, don't go to sleep already," I said. "Tell me a story!"

"What story?" He gulped down the rest of the beer and tossed it on the ground.

"Anything, anything." I tried to think of something interesting. "Tell me about yourself, why are you so quiet all the time?"

"Oh," Keon shrugged. "Rough time back home. It's stuck in my head, man."

He was slowly curling into a ball, but he broke it by lighting a cigarette. It seemed to relax him.

"Why, what do you mean?"

"My family," he paused, as if he was uncertain if he should continue. Then he said, "my family was killed."

"Most of mine too," I told him. "Y-Yôhan's all I got left. If Kowalski was here, he'd say you aren't any different from the rest of us."

"But you..." he paused again and then looked at me with turgid eyes. "You didn't kill them."

"Huh?"

"They lined up my mom and dad," he said. "Gave me a pistol. Told me to choose one or the other."

A chill ran down my spine. The alcohol seemed to fade as he kept telling me the story. I placed myself in his shoes almost. I saw the burning village, the dead bodies—everything that was so familiar to me. And then the man gave me a gun, and told me to choose who lives or who dies. I imagined the man and woman to be my parents. Imagined their nervous eyes. Imagined my dad was telling me to take his life. Imagined my mother sobbing, tears flowing down her face. And then Keon said, "It didn't matter. They killed them both anyway."

I shook my head, trying to get the pictures out of my mind. Thankfully, Y-Yôhan and Ross stumbled back in, using their shirts as pouches to hold numerous beer cans in.

I told Y-Yôhan to toss me one and I immediately drowned myself in its cold liquid. I wanted to get away from what Keon had told me. Pretended like it never happened.

"I think I'm going to bed," Keon said, standing up. "I'll see you in the morning."

Morning. I thought to myself. *I'll have to tell Y-Yôhan this in the morning.* "Goodnight Keon." I waved after him as he walked out of the tent. I popped open another can.

"You know what I don't get?" Y-Yôhan asked.

"What's that?" Ross shot back.

"Why those stupid officers pulled all of us back to Saigon." Y-Yôhan laughed at nothing. "We were fine around Buôn Ma Thuột. Isn't that right, Y-Ben?"

I nodded. I promised myself I wouldn't let what Keon had just told me affect my night. I told myself I'd forget the images I had conjured up in my head. "Yeah, Now we're stuck with people like," I stuck my finger in Ross' face, "You!"

"You know you love me!" Ross playfully pushed me.

"You're going to take that from him, Y-Ben?" Y-Yôhan chuckled.

I shook my head. "Whatever, I'm tired."

"Tired? What a *wuss.*" Ross grinned.

His face was red, and the way his two large front teeth poked out when he smiled seemed so comical in the hazy light of the moon.

"What did you say?" I asked.

"I said you're a *wuss¸* a pansy, a mama's boy!" he shouted.

The ground seemed to sway as I jumped at Ross. He kicked me off, and I fell on my back. He stood over me, begging me to get up back. "C'mon, let's go big boy," Ross said. He struggled to gain his balance like I did. "You want some of this sugah?"

I bull-rushed him at full speed, and tackled his legs. He sprung back and dropped all his bodyweight on top of me. I groaned and jabbed him hard in his side. He retaliated by yanking my arm behind my back.

The marines hollered and cheered. "Show'em, Gunny!"

"You're facin' the Kansas Stallion!" Ross shouted.

I rolled onto my back, and he pinned me down. Out of the corner of my eye, I saw Y-Yôhan running over at us. "Incoming mortar!" Y-Yôhan shouted as he landed on top of us. Ross yelped in shock and slid off me, laughing so hard he keeled over and puked in the dirt. I waited for him to stop and then jumped on his back. He swore, almost landing face-first in his pile of regurgitated steak.

"Kansas Stallion meets the 'yard monkies!" The shouts from the marines never stopped. The screams of "woo hoos" floated through the cool air. Laughter and cheers. Then, a *crack*. The marines dove on the ground and covered their heads. The laughter stopped.

"The heck was that?" Ross asked.

"Frag?" a marine whispered. Frags were becoming common. If a higher grade officer pissed off a grunt, he might find an M-26 grenade rolled under his cot that night.

"That was a gun," Y-Yôhan said.

I looked around. The base would've been pitch black, were it not for the lights around the barracks. I needed to get to my weapon. "Y-Yôhan, we need to get to the barracks."

We moved out, Ross following close behind. I stumbled a couple of times. It could've been the beer. The lights pierced my eyes and cut into my brain. I covered my eyes. "Where's our barracks?" I asked Ross.

"Up north somewhere," he hiccupped.

Our boots scraped across the ground as we scurried toward the barracks. Other soldiers had come out of their quarters with weapons, looking around cautiously. We came to a fork in the road.

"Which way?" I asked Ross.

"Uh, I don't know." He paused. "Split up."

He took the left route, and I continued straight. Y-Yôhan stumbled right. Tree branches whipped pass my face. I tripped over a root and fell in the dirt. I groaned. *No, no, we're under attack, get up!* I spat on the ground and managed to get to my feet, using the walls of one of the barracks to support myself. I couldn't tell if it was ours, but I hoped it was.

I remember seeing blood in the doorway. As I stepped around the corner, a corpse lay sprawled on the ground in its blood. Two silver bars were etched into the man's shoulder-pads. I recognized him as Captain Greer, Ross' platoon leader. I spotted a bloodied K-bar next to his body.

Keon sat quivering in the corner. He had a .44 Magnum pressed against his head. His eyes were wide. Sweat dripped from his brow, mixing in with the blood splattered across his face. There was a jagged wound across his chest. "He tried to take it away from me," he said. "He said he was going to slit my throat if I didn't give it to him."

"Keon, put the gun down," I said. I didn't realize I was walking closer and closer.

"Maybe it's better," he warned, pulling the lever back on the revolver, "if I just get it over with. So I won't have to see anymore dead."

I stepped forward.

"Stop moving!" he warned.

I tried to, but I couldn't find my footing. My vision became hazy and I staggered toward him.

I watched him pulled the trigger.

Crack.

I picked up a can of beer near one of the tents and stuffed it in a plastic trash bag. It fluttered in the wind. My head was screaming at me. My stomach was churning, but I kept moving, picking up the cans.

"You don't have to do that, you know," Y-Yôhan said. He was toying with his necklace, the gems glimmering in the morning sun.

I grunted. "I could've stopped him."

"No one knew—"

"*I did,*" I spat. "I was going to get him someone to talk to..." I stomped on a beer can and stuffed it into the bag.

"Don't blame yourself." Y-Yôhan cleared his throat.

I didn't say anything. I wanted to blame someone else. But I couldn't. There was no one else to point fingers at. It seemed as if the blood of two men were on my hands.

The sun rose over the base, and the clouds began to stretch over the horizon. None of the Americans cared about Keon. They would've spat on his name if they found out that he had killed Captain Greer. He wouldn't even get a chance.

I sat down in a wooden chair, a cup of coffee in my hand. I drank it slowly, the warm liquid rushing down my throat. It was soothing. It made me feel like I was in a longhouse back home in Buôn Alê. Marines walked by. They glared at me.

Ross squatted next to me, elbows resting on his knees. Dark bags drooped from his bloodshot eyes. His voice sounded hoarse when he said, "How you holding up?"

I shrugged. "Alright." The wind howled.

"I'm sorry about Keon."

"It's not Keon," I said. "I didn't even know him. I could've stopped him if I wasn't..." I stopped.

"Drunk?" Ross asked. "You were just living."

I rested the cup on a table next to the chair. I watched the warm brown liquid swivel in the cup. Spinning.

9

I looked at the computer screen, frowning as the Internet browser failed to connect to the website. Couldn't pay the bill again, I thought to myself.

My son wasn't too happy about it. He stormed in my room and asked, "Why can't they just cut off the cellphones instead of the internet? I have to finish a research paper."

I knew that secretly he just wanted to play his online games. "Relax," I said. "You have to learn to live without it. I'll take you to the library or something. You won't die."

"You don't know that," he groaned. "There's nothing to do now."

"Go outside or something. Don't you have friends?" I joked.

"Dad, my generation revolves around games. Without them, there's nothing left."

I laughed. "Trust me, you'll know when that's true."

April 26, 1975

I watched the silhouettes of several choppers float out of the rising sun. I stood with Y-Yôhan and a handful of marines on the edge of the helipad. We used our hands as visors to shield us from the light as we watched the bird land, the rotor wash kicking up sand and dust. The whine of the bird's engine slowly faded as the propellers died down.

Kowalski stepped off the lead bird, grinning. He took the cigarette from his mouth and tossed it on the ground. He was clean shaven, his jacket and trousers freshly creased; though the bags under his eyes showed he hadn't gotten a good night's sleep in days. He was greeted by several marines, including Ross, who gave him a firm handshake and a slap on the back. "Y-Brick! Y-Yôhan!" he called to us.

We couldn't help but smile. The officers at the base had to call Kowalski in early because of the situation with Keon, and always the outstanding marine, he didn't complain. I shook Kowalski's hand and then embraced him. I noticed a new patch on his shoulder. "Staff Sergeant, huh?" I laughed.

Kowalski's flashed a proud smile. "Heck yes, boys. Staff Sergeant Eric Kowalski is back on base."

"Glad to see you." Y-Yôhan's smile faded. "Things haven't been going well."

"So I hear." Kowalski grimaced. "But let's not kill the moment here. I'm starving."

I heard the steak tasted good that day. I cut a piece and pushed it around on my plate.

"America sucks," Kowalski said. "That's why I didn't give a crap when they called me back."

"Why?" I asked.

Kowalski shoved a piece of steak in his mouth and swallowed it without chewing. "Atlanta, Georgia—ever heard of it?"

"Nope," Y-Yôhan admitted.

"Big city. Anyway—I get home, and the whole house is empty. Pictures, silverware, TV, furniture, everything gone."

"Someone break in?" Y-Yôhan asked.

"Worse," Kowalski spat. "Girlfriend left. Sold everything and moved in with some hick from Kentucky."

It's a little embarrassing to admit, but Y-Yôhan and I never had a girlfriend. So we couldn't understand Kowalski's pain, but we could see it in the way he pushed the bloody steak around on his plate, the way his eyes shifted over the entire camp.

"I'm sorry," I said after an awkward silence.

"I expected it, really," he said. "I almost knew, and I still took R&R."

"You needed a break," Y-Yôhan said.

"Naw, I don't need any breaks." Kowalski looked up at us and relaxed his shoulders. "I'm thinkin' about just settling down with the marines for the rest of my life. You know," he began. "Live and die in the corps. Like my pops, and grandpops."

We pushed our steaks around on our plates, too. We weren't hungry anymore.

"So they called you here without me, huh?" Kowalski changed the subject. "Them officers got a lotta nerve."

"Yeah," Y-Yôhan said. "They moved us out of a village near Buôn Ma Thuột and brought us here."

"Didn't give a reason?"

"They're transferring a lot of troops here."

Kowalski bit his lip and finished his steak in one gulp. "The gooks are pushin'."

"That's what I was thinking," I said, secretly proud that I was right. "No one's said anything."

"Well, I'll talk to some of them today to see if I can find out anything," Kowalski said. "Though these boot lieutenants probably wouldn't know crap if it was spoonfed to'em, so don't expect much."

I smiled. "Alright, we'll go have a talk with the squad."

Kowalski left the table, after downing a glass of water, and headed toward the officer tents at the back of the base. We watched him slap a few marines on the shoulder and teased them, with a crooked grin.

"Hey, you look tired," Y-Yôhan said, nodding at the bags beneath my eyes.

"Yeah, I might try and take a nap or something." I stretched and yawned.

"You should," he laughed. "You look like someone raised you from the dead."

"Does it really?" I groaned and rubbed my eyes. I hadn't slept in two nights. The officers didn't have any other barracks for us to sleep in, so after they carried Keon and Captain Greer's bodies out in ponchos, we had to try and ignore the bloodstains on the wall.

The sky was a starless. I left the snoring squad, quietly slipping away through the door. I coughed into my balled fist and made my way to the cafeteria, where it was brighter and lights were strung from the corners of the tents.

I laid down on one of the tables outside, wet from a light drizzle of rain hours ago. I took a deep breath and stared up into the darkness. I heard the voices of my cousins, shouting at me to jump from the waterfall long ago. I felt the explosions that rippled through the earth that Chinese New Year. I saw the woman that used to make me steamed mung beans. I saw the hole in her head.

"You can sleep inside, you know?" a voice echoed from the darkness. Kowalski was walking towards me, the scent of his cigarette drifting in the air.

I chuckled. "Yeah, I know."

He sat down at a table next to mine and puffed a cloud of smoke. "Can't sleep?"

"Can you?" I replied.

"Nope," he said.

"Me neither, then." I crossed my arms and watched the nothing in the sky. Then there was a cold silence, as I watched his clouds of bluish smoke drift upward.

"So Ross got you guys messed up, I hear." He looked at me.

"Yeah. Wish he hadn't."

"Because of Keon?"

I nodded.

"I don't got any sympathy to feed ya," Kowalski said.

I smiled. "I was kind of hoping you would say that."

"Guess you've been with me too long." He said. "Starting to read my mind."

"Well, you guys need us, right?" I cursed the words before slipped from my mouth.

"I need ya'll?" Kowalski asked, he leaned forward, an elbow resting on his knee.

"Nevermind." But I knew it was too late to take it back now.

"The U.S. Army don't need you 'yards," he said, raising his voice slightly. "That's not my opinion. That's a matter of fact."

I sat up and faced up. "I didn't mean it like that."

"Let me finish, Y-Brick." He tossed the cigarette butt on the ground and kicked some dirt over it. "The U.S. Army might not need you, but I've seen what them gooks are doin' to your land, what *we're* doing to it. That's why I recruited you."

"Oh," was all I could say.

"Ya see, command wanted us to run recon to defend *our* bases in the Central Highlands," he said. "*I* did it to defend ya'll." He sighed. "Look, before I was in command of you 'yards, I was a squad leader in a platoon led by this Lieutenant Briggs. We were ambushed at one of our firebases near Buôn Ma Thuột. We would've been fried if you guys didn't come outta nowhere."

I turned my eyes to the dark of the sky. The name Briggs made me shiver. "Briggs—I think I knew him."

"Heh, how?"

"I watched him die." I took a deep breath. Images of the dead ran through my mind in an obscure haze. I couldn't escape death.

"Hmph." Kowalski lit another cigarette. He was obviously surprised. "I take it you fought with him?"

"If you call a little thirteen-year-old spraying an M16 'fighting'."

"See, that's just it," he said. "That's why I love you guys. The 'yards I mean. Because you guys are born warriors. The big ol' patriot types in our army don't know what it's like to watch their countrymen burn in their homes."

I nodded. "They don't know what it's like to fight a losing fight for their homeland."

"Exactly." Kowalski blew a cloud of smoke over my head.

"Kowalski."

"Yeah?"

"Do you believe in God?"

Kowalski crossed his arms. "I mean, I guess. Why?"

I looked back up to the sky and saw a light. *A plane,* I thought. Silence filled the air, and the light didn't move. It just glowed brighter, ever brighter. *A star.* "God," I said. "He's all we've got left."

10

It seemed like any other day. My wife was at work, and it was the summertime. I expected my son to be gone already, one of his friends picking him up. So it came as a surprise when my son approached as I was fixing a cup of coffee to drink with the French bread and brie cheese.

"Hey dad?"

"Hmm?" I asked while sipping from the cup.

"When did you come to America?"

"Seventy-five," I said almost instantly.

"Anything special happen?" he asked. "Shoot more guns? Ride an elephant?"

"Nah," I smiled. "It was very hectic though—Kowalski and Ross were always arguing. But we all made it out fine."

"How about Y-Yôhan?" he asked.

I smiled, remembering. "No," I said. "No, he didn't."

April 26, 1975

Explosions shattered the morning. I awoke, finding myself still lying on the table, the sun beaming down on my face. I looked around; all around me soldiers raced from building to building, some of them already armed. Minutes later I spotted jeeps pulling out, kicking up dirt as they sped out into Saigon's streets.

I found Kowalski in the barracks. Men were pulling on their equipment and checking their weapons. "What's going on?"

"Gooks are making a push," he said, shaking his head. "We're not prepared for this."

Y-Yôhan put a hand on my shoulder and squeezed. I looked into his cold, brown eyes.

I understood. This was the only part of Vietnam left. If it fell, there'd be nothing left. A part of me was wondering why the U.S. couldn't spare more troops. From what every marine seemed to believe, they had enough people to take out Vietnam, Cambodia and Laos without breaking a sweat. I grabbed my weapon and headed out with the rest of the squad. A couple of other men followed behind us, from a different platoon—one was Ross, striding slowly to us, his eyes still adjusting to the sunlight.

"Hold your horses, Sarge," a man spoke gruffly from behind us. We turned to see a lieutenant standing tall, a rifle strapped to his back. "It was just some gook rockets."

"What's your point?" Kowalski growled.

"Son, you better watch your tone, or I swear you'll regret it." The lieutenant's eyes were steel. "There's nothing out there to fight."

"Sir, Saigon hasn't been hit with anything for almost four years," Ross said. "You're tellin' me 'just some gook rockets' ain't something to worry about?"

"You sit here and the whole city will fall," Kowalski spat. A vein emerged from his neck, and he turned red.

"Lieutenant, sir!" A young soldier with round, thick glasses emerged from a nearby tent. "Captain wants to talk with you."

The lieutenant didn't move his eyes from Kowalski. He stood as tall and was a little bigger, but even that did not dull the fierceness in Kowalski's eyes. "Do *not* move. That's an order." He went through the flaps of the tent.

Kowalski swore and kicked a beer can across the ground. "...boot lieutenant couldn't even hit a gook if he was humpin' its back."

"The heck we doin', Eric?" Ross asked.

"You heard the man," Kowalski said. He mockingly added, "They're just some gook rockets."

I grimaced. The rockets themselves might've not been a great concern. Saigon was a very large city—the rockets could've hit many vacant buildings— but then again, it could've struck somewhere troops were set up.

"They have way more men then we do, and the army knows it," Kowalski said. "They come bargin' into the city, and we'll be overrun in an hour."

"We don't have enough troops to push out," Y-Yôhan stated. "We'll get crushed."

Kowalski reached for a cigarette, but stopped when the lieutenant stormed from the tent.

"Sarge—Gunny—get your men to the landing strip," he said walking up to us. "They need everyone there pronto."

"What?" Kowalski spat. "They want us to run with our tails between our legs like some dogs? You know what them gooks do to dogs? They *eat them*."

"Do as you're told, Sarge," the lieutenant barked. "Now get to the strip, or I'll see you court-martialed."

I could feel Kowalski's temper rising, and I slapped his shoulder and pulled him back a little.

"Don't worry, Y-Brick. I ain't low enough to hit a pile of crap like this guy," he snarled. "Let's go."

We made our way to the strip. Kowalski was unnervingly quiet. The squad followed behind us. None of us wanted to leave, but it was certain death if we didn't. I noticed Y-Yôhan kept rubbing the gems on his pendant nervously. He kept looking back over his shoulder, as if something was chasing him. At that time, I didn't know what.

The landing strip had a huge plane. It was being fueled, and civilians rushed to get a seat. Men, women, and children were shouting and yelling, hoping to get in. A half-dozen large helicopters landed and took off, carrying as many as they could.

We approached the man in charge, a Captain who was trying to get a frequency on the radio. We could hear a Vietnamese voice on the other end, cursing at the Americans. The Captain swore in frustration and shouted, "Somebody get me a dang frequency!"

"Captain," Kowalski said, clearing his throat.

"What is it?" he asked, turning to look at us. "Jesus, Sarge, why are them 'yards here?"

"Why *aren't* they here? These are my men," Kowalski said. "We were told to come here for evac."

The Captain shook his head and blinked. "God—alright, put'em in a chopper or something."

"Where's it going?" Ross asked.

"One of the aircraft carriers, then probably the Carolinas," the Captain said. "Honestly I could care less—just get the men in there so we don't have shells blowing up our birds."

Adrenaline rushed through my body. At the same time, I was excited. For what—I couldn't grasp. Here we were, brothers through the war, fighting for everything we had. Our home, our families—and now we were running. Like Kowalski said, we were running like dogs with our tails between our legs. Scared and helpless. But that's why we *had* to run. We couldn't win. We couldn't.

Kowalski boarded the helicopter first. It was a Chinook, I recognized, with propellers on each end. I could smell the inside of the cabin, reeking of sweat and urine. It brought back nostalgia of dropping into reconnaissance. The blades began to whir, and the engine roared to life. I followed after Kowalski, and a couple of the squad did as well. I turned to the back of the chopper and looked for Y-Yôhan. He wasn't there.

I stepped to the door of the chopper and saw a few men still climbing it. Beyond them, I saw several soldiers, their eyes falling on the mountains in the distance. The land they had called home all their life was being taken away from them. I watched in silence, until I realized Y-Yôhan was among them. His M16 rested on his shoulder, and his hair fluttered in the rotor wash of the bird. He lit a cigarette and puffed smoke toward the mountains, which dissipated as soon as they left his lips. I saw him reaching for something at his neck, but it was hard to see in the glare of the sun.

"Y-Yôhan!" I shouted through cupped hands. "Let's go!"

He turned, his eyes planted on his feet as he stepped toward the Chinook. He approached slowly, his boots shuffling against the ground. I reached out my hand to help him in. He hesitated, and then took my hand and shook it. I felt something between our hands, solid and rough. Dread washed over my body as he took a deep breath and looked up at me.

"Take care of it, and I'll take care of home," he said, squeezing my hand.

One gaze into his eyes made me understand. He let go of my hand and I stared down into my palm and saw green and purple gems hanging loosely from his copper necklace. My throat tightened. "You're staying?"

He grinned—the grin he sported when he leapt from the waterfall and when he told me the story of his first kill. The grin that hated monkeys and wrestled drunk. "This will always be home to me. But you have to go," he shouted over the whistle of the Chinook.

"This is my home too!" I yelled back. "You don't remember the deal we made when we were kids?"

"Someone has to tell our story, Y-Ben," he said, stepping closer. He put a hand on my shoulder and said, "You were always the better storyteller." His eyes never moved from mine. The way he stood, so proud and tall, made me realize there was nothing I could say to change his mind.

"We've got to get out of here before they drop another shell on us!" the pilot shouted from the cockpit. "Hurry it up!"

I looked at the pilot and then back to Y-Yôhan. "You better make it to America, *ayong*." Older brother.

"I will," he replied. We embraced, and he patted my back. "Promise."

I watched him step away, the rifle slung over his shoulder. The Chinook slowly ascended, climbing into the sky. Y-Yôhan saluted. His smile never faded. Kowalski and I saluted back, and soon, he was nothing more than a speck in the distance.

"He's really stayin' huh?" Kowalski was lighting a cigarette.

I was still looking out the window, my eyes drifting over the shore. Vietnam was falling behind, and soon, we were flying over the top of the dark blue waters of the Pacific. "Yeah," I said. I looked down to Y-Yôhan's pendant in my hand, and slid the gems around. The green and purple seemed to shine so brightly in the sun.

"Don't worry. He'll be safe there," the pilot said from the front seat. "U.S. said they'll evacuate the 'yards out."

I knew better. I would've stayed if I could've. I would've stayed and fought until my blood ran down the rivers of the highlands, and mixed with the tears of my ancestors. But Y-Yôhan gave me a task, and I wouldn't die until someone heard our story. About our lives.

Our people. Our homeland.

11

June 6, 2010

The lights dimmed, and the crowd grew silent. My eyes quickly adjusted to the darkness of the auditorium, and soon, lights from the fly gallery filled the stage. Several students held instruments in their hands, including my son, who sat, grinning at his drum set, dressed in a red gown and cap.

The audience cheered as the band began to play a soothing blues and jazz mixture. I watched my son laugh and shout, spinning his drumsticks between his fingers and slapping away at the drums. It was nice to see him put so much enthusiasm in something productive for once. My wife raised her camera, and I heard the *click* of the shutter.

The audience applauded—hooted and hollered—then the curtains closed. The principal of the school and other teachers and officials came to join him at the podium. He was obviously proud of this moment, from the way his face was stretched into a wide grin.

After a short speech, they began to hand diplomas out. A line of red and gold cap and gowns stretched in the darkness off-stage. My wife struggled to find my son. I assumed he was putting his drumset away.

"Don't worry, you'll see him," I said over the shouts of the people in front of me. I grabbed her hand and squeezed. As much as it would be a blessing to see our son graduate, it would be difficult to watch him go. I knew the dangers of the world better than anyone, and I had a creeping feeling that somehow, someway, he'd get caught up in the wrong crowd.

My wife wriggled her hand from my grip and playfully smacked me. "Why were you squeezing so hard?"

I shook my head. "Sorry, I'm thinking too much." I looked out into the crowd. My son was next in line. He had never stopped smiling. "Hey, hey," I patted my wife's lap and motioned to her camera, "He's going next. Take pictures."

The student in front of him danced across stage to the shouts and applause of his family and friends and shook the hands of the principal and teachers and took the diploma. I could only imagine what they must feel like.

Then, my son stepped forward. "Y-Yako Niehrah," the principal read
out, his name echoing throughout the stadium. He was met with thunderous
applause from his classmates. I managed to hear the shutter of my wife's camera
flickering as she snapped pictures. I wouldn't be surprised if they all turned out
blurry. He turned to his class and bowed to them jokingly, met by grins and
chuckles from his classmates. He grabbed the principal's hand to shake, and
then hugged him, patting him on the back.

My wife was laughing. "He's crazy," she said.

Y-Yako joined his classmates on the wooden bleachers, and he looked
over at us. I waved my hand, and he gave a half-salute. I smiled and saluted back.

"So how does it feel to graduate?" Mrs. Scott asked Y-Yako across the
table. The Scotts were close family friends—Y-Yako and their son Jake practi-
cally grew up together.

"Great," Y-Yako said, shoving a spoonful of rice into his mouth. The
noises of clattering plates and loud whispers filled the air. The buffet line was
full, and I had gotten enough to last me the entire day.

"What are you thinking about for college?" Mrs. Scott asked.

"He wants to write video games," Jake said, ripping the top of the paper
from his straw and blowing it in Y-Yako's face.

"Jake," Mr. Scott warned. "Manners."

"Yeah, *manners*," Y-Yako subtlety mocked. He looked back over to Mrs.
Scott and said, "I'm doing something with English—after that, I really don't
know."

"Well, you could always teach," my wife said.

"Eh, I think I'd be a bad teacher," he replied.

"Got that right," Jake mumbled.

"I want to publish a couple of books too," Y-Yako said. "I think I might
try to get one done over this summer before college starts up."

"Oh, what's it going to be about?" Mr. Scott asked after swallowing what
seemed to be a painful lump of mashed potatoes and hibachi.

"I think I'm going to write something on the Montagnards," Y-Yako
said. I looked up from my plate, and he was looking directly at me for a second,
then he turned his attention elsewhere.

"If you do that, I can help you," I said.

"I think I got a lot already," he said, grinning. "I've already written a couple of pages.

"Where are you getting stories?" I asked. "Some sites, they might have wrong information."

"You, Dad." Y-Yako chuckled. "You think I wasn't listening when you told your stories?"

I sat back in my chair and crossed my arms. *What a kid.*

August 26, 2010

It was move-in day at the college. Y-Yako hadn't packed much. He said he didn't need all these fancy things to live. "Food, working internet, and a toilet are just fine by me," he'd say. Y-Yako and I lugged in the boxes, the heaviest being his computer that looked like it had come from a Star Wars film. My wife made the bed neatly, tucking the sheets in tight.

"Why are you making it so neat?" Y-Yako groaned. "People are going to think I'm nerdier than I already am."

"What is a girl going to come in your room?" my wife asked.

"No, well, I don't know—I don't even know who my roommate is," Y-Yako said. The moment the words left his mouth, a skinny asian boy with a shaved head walked in through the door, a box in his arms. He was turning red.

Y-Yako grabbed the box, and realizing how heavy it was, he gently rested it on the ground. "You my roommate?"

"Depends who's asking," the boy said in a joking southern accent. "Yeah, man. Tyler Lee." He stuck out his hand. I watched Y-Yako chuckle.

He took the hand and shook. "I'm Y-Yako."

"Ee, what?"

"Ee-Yah-Ko," my son repeated slowly.

"Alright, whatever," Rusty said. "I'm going to go get the rest of my stuff, then we can talk some more, alright?"

"Yeah, yeah, sure," Y-Yako said, waving goodbye to his new friend. He turned to us and shrugged.

"I think you'll like it," I said.

"Aw, I'm gonna miss you guys," he teased, running up to his mom and giving her a huge hug. "No stir fry and spring rolls until Thanksgiving, what will I do?"

"Try to cook yourself," she groaned as he squeezed her.

"Don't tempt me," Y-Yako said. He stepped back and then turned to me.

I said the first words. "Study hard now, boy, and stay away from these parties."

"Don't worry, the only parties I'm going to are ones that include video games," he joked.

"And *don't* stay up playing video games all night. You need to concentrate on your studies," my wife pleaded.

"I know, I know," he said.

"Oh yeah," I said, reaching into my pocket. I pulled out a small box wrapped in golden paper. "This is for you."

"Thanks Dad." He took it. "Is it shakeable?"

"No," I said quickly. "Take special care of it—guard it with your life."

Y-Yako laughed and then pretended to look through the box. "Hmm, do I sense, car keys?"

My wife laughed.

"That is a very special gift," I said. "And I think it's about time to give it to you."

"Great, now I'm all excited," Y-Yako said. "Can I open it?"

"Open it tonight," I said. "Midnight."

"Alright," he looked at the both of us, and then finally we embraced.

"Be good," I said.

We left the campus a few minutes later. It was quiet on the highway; the only sound was the distant oldies playing on the radio, my wife's soft breathing, and the rumble of the tires as they rolled over the road. I was wondering what Y-Yako would do when he opened the box and saw green and purple gems swaying from a copper chain.

———

That night, before we went to sleep, we knelt by the bed, closed our eyes and prayed. I never told my wife what I prayed for. I took a deep breath, and let my mind speak for itself.

I told someone our stories, like you wanted me to. I gave Y-Yako your necklace, too—I beg for forgiveness in advance, if he breaks it. I told him to open it tonight—it's your birthday isn't it? I bet they're throwing you a big feast up there. Roasted water buffalo over a bonfire, with plenty to go around. Save some for me, when I get up there, alright? Because I'll probably see you sooner than I think, ayong.

There'll be a time where we'll be able to sling stones and shoot our crossbows across the jungle again. Where we can sit high upon the back of elephants and dive from the top of waterfalls.

I promise.